JOURNEY

SOULLESS KINGS MC: MARBLE FALLS, TX
BOOK 2

ANDI RHODES

BLUE JOURNEY PUBLISHING

Copyright © 2024 by Andi Rhodes

All rights reserved.

No part of this book may be reproduced in any form or by any electronic or mechanical means, including information storage and retrieval systems, without written permission from the author, except for the use of brief quotations in a book review.

This is a work of fiction and the product of the author's imagination. All names, characters, businesses, places, events and incidents are used in a fictitious manner, unless otherwise noted. Any resemblance to actual persons, living or deceased, or actual events is purely coincidental.

Cover Artwork - © Dez Purington at Pretty in Ink Creations

Editing - Darcie Fisher at Into the Gray Author Services

A NOTE FROM THE AUTHOR:

Welcome back Soulless Kings fans! The ride continues with Journey and Wren's story, and I'm stoked that you've decided to read it. I'm not one to give spoilers or divulge too much, but did want to point one thing out for this book. If you don't want to know anything ahead of time, skip the rest of this note!

I have never shied away from difficult or triggering topics, nor have I always felt the need for trigger warnings, but this book does deal with a very complex mental health disorder so I'm kinda chucking my own rules out the window.

Dissociative Identity Disorder, or multiple personalities as you might know it, is very real and not very represented. I did a lot of research, as well as relied on my social work background, for this story, but please keep in mind that it is still a work of fiction. I do take some creative liberties in order to keep the story flowing.

That being said, this is a wild one, and I hope like hell that you love these two (or fourteen) as much as I do!

Much love,
 Andi

"Sometimes, mental illness is terrifying because you feel like you've lost control of your mind and nothing makes sense. It's like watching yourself on autopilot and having little to no control."
-Anonymous

This book is for anyone who has experienced trauma, who's mental health has taken a beating and feels like their lives are spiraling out of control. You are stronger than you think. You are worthy of happiness. You are a survivor, and that's something to be proud of.

Journey...

I've never wanted anything other than to be a patched member of the Soulless Kings MC. And now I'm their VP. Having a title earns me some level of respect and a fairly large amount of women. I'm living the biker dream.

But a one-night stand changes everything because I can't get the woman out of my head. Problem is, when I see her again, she has no clue who I am. In fact, it's almost as if she's a different person. All I know is I want to make her mine.

I'll do anything to convince all of her that we belong together, even if it means walking away from the life I love.

Wren...

Fractured. Broken. Crazy. For as long as I can remember, I've been called all of these and more. Maybe there's something to it though because I've always had long periods of time just... *disappear*. People who swear they've met me are strangers, and those I do recognize treat me like fragile glass.

One particular stranger catches my interest, but he swears we know each other. When he starts to show up at all the same places as me, all my internal alarms go off. The man is relentless, and after a while, I begin to look for him everywhere I go.

I'm certain I could never fit into his world, but maybe, just maybe, he can make some changes to fit into mine.

PROLOGUE
WREN

I hate the dark.

Five years old…

"Sonofabitch!"

My eyes widen, and I cover my mouth with my hand as I watch Daddy hop around on one foot. Mommy told me to clean up my toys, but I couldn't find one of Barbie's shoes. I guess it was hiding in the carpet.

"Wren!" Daddy shouts when he finally stops acting like a jumping bean and stares at the ceiling. "Get your ass down here!"

I scoot further behind the couch toward the corner. I've learned to make myself invisible when Daddy's mad, and right now, he's really really mad.

"I'm gonna count to three," he yells. "And if you're n—"

"Keep your voice down," Mommy snaps, and I stand to peer over the furniture as she walks into the living room. "I just got Ry down for his nap."

Daddy stomps toward Mommy and leans down so his nose is almost touching hers. "I'll yell if I goddamn wanna yell," he snarls.

Mommy lowers her head and mumbles an apology. When she turns to walk back into the kitchen, Daddy grabs her arm and spins her around to face him again.

"Don't you dare walk away from me," he barks.

When crying fills the air, I glance at the ceiling. So much for Ryan's naptime.

"Go shut that baby up," Daddy snaps, punctuating his demand with a slap across Mommy's face.

Without thinking, I jump out from behind the couch and run to Mommy. "Leave her alone!" I shout as I throw my arms around her legs.

"Baby, it's okay," Mommy says. "Go upstairs. I'll be up in a minute."

I shake my head, and Daddy scowls. "Do as you're told."

"I'm not lea—"

Pain radiates through my head when Daddy's hand connects with my cheek. I fall to the floor and scramble to my place behind the couch. Someone must turn the lights off because it gets dark, and I'm scared.

I hate the dark.

"Can you hear me?"

"Jesus, what the hell happened here?"

I squint against the light shining in my eyes. "Mommy?"

"What's your name, honey?"

"She's in shock. Take her to the EMTs and have her checked out."

A man I don't recognize lifts me from the floor and curls his hand at the back of my head, gently pushing my face into his shoulder.

"Mommy?"

"It's okay honey. You're safe."

I feel safe. But I still want my mommy. Propping my chin on his shoulder, I watch as strangers move back and forth in the living room, from one red pile of clothes to another. My eyes lock on the smallest pile and the tiny hand sticking out from under it.

Before I can figure out which of my dolls it belongs to, the darkness swallows me whole.

CHAPTER 1
JOURNEY

Dibs.

Present day…

"Fuck, I thought this day would never end."

I slowly turn to face Jackyl, our club doc, who's locking the front door of the club-owned free clinic after the last patient leaves. I've been waiting on him for two hours because he doesn't know how to say 'no' to anyone who walks through the door needing his help.

"You're kidding right?" I counter. "We coulda been five beers in by now if you would've told Mrs. Kuntz that she's a hypochondriac instead of listening to her go on and on about how she's convinced she's got testicular cancer."

Jackyl chuckles. "If we had a good head-shrinker in town, I'd refer her." He shrugs. "But for now, I'm all the people of Marble Falls have."

"Jesus, I don't envy you."

"Which is why the first round's on you."

Twenty minutes later, I hand the bartender at Ballinger's Bar a fifty to start a tab before carrying two beers and two shots to the corner of the bar where Jackyl is standing. He's scanning the crowd, no doubt looking for a pussy to lose himself in tonight.

"Any possibilities?" I ask.

"It's still early."

"If you wanna get your dick wet, you could've done that at the clubhouse," I remind him.

"Club whores are a dime a dozen." He downs the shot of Jack before smirking. "Besides, I had Molly last night. I'm in the mood for a change."

I follow suit and set my empty glass on the closest table. Jackyl's not wrong, but hitting up the bars in town isn't exactly a sure thing. Especially on a weeknight when the pickin's are slim.

"Well, whatever happens tonight, we need to be ready to ride tomorrow morning," I tell him. "Crow wants us on the road by nine."

"Pres really thinks all of us need to go?"

"You know how he is when it comes to his old

lady. Addison's presenting at that law enforcement conference, and he's not letting her out of his sight for that long."

"Fuckin' hell," he bites out, shoving a hand through his hair. "Surrounded by bacon isn't exactly how I want to spend the rest of my week."

"Me either, but what Pres wants, Pres gets."

As the Soulless Kings MC vice president, I tried to reason with Crow. I reminded him that Addi is a cop, and she'll be surrounded by cops so there's no need for him to go all out for protection. And he threw back at me that it was a dirty cop who fucked up her life to begin with. Hard to argue with that.

Before the conversation can go any further, Jackyl's attention diverts to the entrance, and he whistles.

"Well, well, well… Looks like our night just got infinitely better."

I follow his gaze and practically swallow my tongue at the sight of the two women standing just inside the door. The taller one is a beautiful blonde, but it's the shorter one who catches my eye.

She's average height with dark brown hair and dressed in tight jeans, black leather boots, and a tank that shows off the tattoos on her arms and shoulders.

"Dibs on the brunette," Jackyl says as he takes a step in their direction.

I grab his arm to stop him, and he glances over his shoulder. "Dibs."

"Aw, c'mon, brother," he whines.

"I outrank you." I shrug. "So… dibs."

"Seriously?" Jackyl scowls. "You're gonna pull that card on me?"

I grin. "Yep."

Dropping his arm, I push past him and move toward the women. Before I can reach them, a man in jeans and a hoodie blocks my path and strikes up a conversation with the ladies. I watch as the women laugh at something he says, but then the brunette's expression shifts, and the hairs on the back of my neck stand on end.

"Not interested," she says, loud enough to be heard over the music.

"C'mon, baby," he cajoles. "You know you want me."

"She said no," the blonde snaps.

"Wasn't talking to you, bitch."

"Excuse me?" Blondie demands, hands on her hips.

"You're fuckable," he says matter-of-factly. "But it's her pants I wanna get in."

Rage burns my veins, and I grab the guy by the shoulder and yank him back. "The lady said she wasn't interested," I snarl.

Blondie smirks, but it's not her reaction I'm interested in. I level my gaze on the sexy brunette, and she blushes.

The guy looks from them to me and back again. "Sorry," he mutters before yanking out of my hold and stomping away.

"We had it handled," Blondie says, her smirk disappearing.

I lift my hands in surrender. "Okay."

"Yo, J!" I glance over my shoulder at Jackyl and see him walking toward us. "Ya gonna introduce me or what?"

Rolling my eyes, I return my gaze to the women. "Ladies, this is Jackyl, and I'm Journey," I say. "And Jackyl, this is…" I pointedly stare at them, hoping they'll fill in the blanks for me.

"I'm Leah," Blondie says. "And she's Wren," she continues with a nod at her friend.

"Wren," I repeat, savoring the way her name rolls off my tongue.

"Why don't you ladies let us buy you a drink?" Jackyl suggests.

Leah and Wren exchange a look before Wren shrugs and returns her focus to me. "Sounds good."

Grinning, I turn toward the bar. "Follow me."

CHAPTER 2
WREN

CAN YOU FUCK AWAY MY DEMONS?

FOLLOW ME.

Two very simple words, but the physical reaction my body is experiencing to them is anything but. My stomach flutters like it's holding a million butterflies, and my heart pounds so hard I fear it'll explode right out of my chest.

I'd fucking follow this man anywhere... Especially if that ass is on display.

Leah leans close to me. "Close your mouth before the drool starts dripping to the floor," she whispers.

I whip my head to the left and stare at her with wide eyes. "What?"

"You're staring," she informs me. "And you're

starting to walk funny from pressing your thighs together."

"I have no clue what you're talking about," I reply indignantly, shifting my eyes forward.

"Bullshit." Leah giggles. "If we weren't in public, you'd already be fucking the man."

Journey hesitates mid-step, and his shoulders shake with laughter before he continues forward.

"Could you be any louder?" I ask Leah, my whisper harsh.

"I don't mind," Journey says without turning around.

Heat floods my cheeks, and I groan.

"What'll you have?" Journey asks when we reach the bar.

"Vodka cranberry."

"Gin and tonic."

Leah and I speak simultaneously, and Journey nods before rattling off our order to the bartender.

Once our drinks are presented, a few minutes of silence pass while we all dive in. Jackyl strikes up a conversation with Leah, and it's not long before the two disappear onto the dancefloor.

"Wanna dance?" Journey asks me. I shake my head, and he sighs with relief. "Thank fuck. I can't dance for shit."

Chuckling, I smile at him. "Me either. At least not

—" Realizing what I was about to say, I slap a hand over my mouth.

Journey's eyes spark with curiosity, and he gently grabs my hand and lowers it to my side. "At least not what?"

"Vertically," I blurt, somehow recognizing that he's not going to let me off the hook. "I can't dance vertically."

He arches a brow. "Is that so?"

I square my shoulders. "Yep."

Now, this behavior might cause some to think I'm a slut, and maybe they'd be right. But the truth of the matter is, I like sex. It's the one thing I can do that chases away my demons. Sure, it's temporary, but it's also the closest to perfection someone like me can get, so why not indulge when I can?

He downs the shot of Jack he ordered before grabbing my hand. "How 'bout you show me?"

I slip my hand out of his grip. "I don't even know you."

Not that that is gonna actually stop me.

Journey's eyes darken. "That's an easy fix," he says. "Whaddya wanna know?"

Can you fuck away my demons?

"Journey and Jackyl," I say instead. "What kinda names are those?"

"They're road names," he says. "Ya know… for bikers."

"I'm sure there's a story there."

"There is," he confirms. "But is storytime really what you're after?"

I grin. "Nope."

"Next question."

I glance at his hand. "Are you single, or do you have a ring tucked away somewhere?"

Journey stiffens as if I've offended him. "If I were taken, I wouldn't be here hoping like hell that you're gonna stop playing twenty questions and ask me to take you home."

"Fair enough."

"So?"

I pause for a moment, liking the back-and-forth banter with him. "What's your favorite position?"

His lips tilt upward. "Whatever position gets you off."

My pussy clenches with desperation, and I brush past him and head for the door. Glancing over my shoulder, I ask, "You comin'?"

I don't bother waiting. He'll follow.

As soon as I step outside, I move to my right and pull my cell out of my back pocket to send a quick text to Leah to let her know I'm leaving.

"I'm this way."

My gaze whips to Journey, and his thumb is hitched over his shoulder.

"Yeah, I'm gonna drive myself," I tell him.

He shrugs. "Suit yourself."

I rattle off my address and continue to my car. Ten minutes later, I'm pulling into the parking lot of my apartment building, and Journey is behind me on his Harley.

"Nice place," Journey comments after I get out of my car.

I look around at our surroundings, taking in where I live and trying to see it from his perspective. The smell from the overflowing dumpster pollutes the air, and the piles of broken furniture are an eyesore. The building itself is rundown, as are the vehicles filling the lot.

I face Journey and smirk. "Not a fan of liars."

He chuckles, and the deep rumble renews the lust he evoked back at the bar. "How about politeness?"

Pretending to think about it for a moment, I tap my chin. "Yeah, I think I can deal with that."

"Good."

"C'mon. I promise, it can only go up from here."

"I'm counting on it," he says with a wink.

Leading him to my third-story walkup, my mind races. I've never cared one way or another about others' opinions because they're like assholes…

everyone has one. But I find myself giving a damn about what this man thinks.

When I open my door, I step inside and to the left so he can enter. Holding my breath, I wait for his reaction, and when he whistles, I smile. The outside of my home might be shit, but inside is an entirely different matter.

"I was *not* expecting this," he says as he approaches my wall of art. "Did you do these?"

My eyes flit from one colored-pencil drawing to the next, pride welling in my chest. Life might be challenging for me, but at least I know I excel at something.

"Yeah. I, uh, illustrate children's books. Those are the originals."

"You're really good."

"I know."

"And humble," he teases.

I shrug. "I'm sure there's something you're good at and not at all ashamed to admit it."

He crosses the room to me and grabs my hand to tug me into his chest. "There's a lot I'm good at," he says, heat sparking in his gaze. "And by morning, you'll know exactly how good I am."

Journey dips his head and fuses his lips to mine. He darts his tongue into my mouth, swirling it around mine. He tastes of liquor and sin and smells of leather and smoke.

Yanking my hips forward, he presses his hard cock against me. Electricity zips through my system, and I moan into his mouth.

"Bedroom?" he asks when he pulls his head back.

I shake my head as I slide my hands between our bodies and unbuckle his belt. "Right here."

Journey's nostrils flare. "Fine by me."

He grips the hem of my shirt and lifts it over my head before tossing it to the floor. Then he unsnaps my jeans and shoves them and my panties down. Without warning, he thrusts his hand between my legs and slides a finger between my folds.

"Oh, God," I groan, letting my head fall back.

Journey urges me backward until I connect with the wall. He leans in and latches onto a nipple, not bothering to take off my bra.

"So fucking sexy," he says when he releases me. He pushes two fingers inside me and growls. "So fucking wet."

"Cock," I plead. "I need your cock."

"Not quite yet." He drops to his knees, presses his face to my pussy, and licks my clit. "Sexy, wet, and goddamn sweet."

He crooks his fingers, hitting that elusive spot

deep within, and the combination of that and his mouth causes my hips to buck.

"That's it," he croons. "Come for me, Wren."

The sound of him saying my name does me in, and I convulse around him. He doesn't let up on his ministrations until my knees go weak.

Journey rises to his full height, a grin on his face as he licks his lips. With his stare leveled on me, he strips, and the sound of his erection hitting his stomach seems to echo in the space.

"I'm gonna fill you up," he growls as he lifts me so I can wrap my legs around his waist.

He reaches down to line himself up with my entrance and then pushes inside me in one long, smooth thrust. I stretch to accommodate his impressive size and dig my heels into his back like I'm afraid he's going to pull away.

While Journey undulates his hips, he slips my bra strap from my shoulder to expose my breast before leaning down to suck a nipple between his lips. As he glides in and out of me, I use the wall as leverage to match his pace.

Heat builds from the inside out, and I know this man is gonna make me come a second time in a matter of minutes. When he releases my nipple with a pop, a shiver races down my spine, and I bite my bottom lip as a wave of pleasure washes over me.

"So soon?" he teases.

I nod frantically as my orgasm intensifies, refusing to release me from its grip. Several more thrusts, and Journey's cock pulses. He sinks his teeth into my shoulder, groaning as his movements slow.

My body goes limp, but he doesn't let me go. Instead, he slides out of me and carries me to the couch. After gently laying me down, he walks away, and I'm too spent to wonder where he's going.

When he returns, he presses a warm washcloth between my legs, and I squeak with shock.

"What the fuck?" I ask, although my tone is not nearly as demanding as I'd hoped.

"Shhh," he urges. "Just cleaning you up."

"Oh."

"Get some rest," he says. "We're going another round before I leave."

"Promise?" I ask sleepily.

"Damn straight."

Yawning, I let my eyes fall closed. Within seconds, I'm asleep. That's what sex does to me. It chases the world away and lets me rest.

I don't know how long I sleep, but Journey is a man of his word. We fuck on the couch twice more before I doze off again. And when I wake up, unwelcome annoyance slithers through me.

Journey, along with any trace of him, is gone.

CHAPTER 3
JOURNEY

I'VE GOTTA FIND A WAY TO GET THIS CHICK OUT OF MY HEAD.

"Earth to Journey."

Crow waves his hand in front of my face, and I shake my head to clear it. Ever since I left Wren's apartment in the wee hours of the morning, I haven't been able to get her outta my thoughts.

"Huh?"

Crow frowns. "What the fuck is going on with you?"

"Nothing."

"Bull," he snaps. "You've been zoned out since we left the clubhouse."

"Yeah, Journey," Jackyl taunts as he comes up behind me and slaps my back. "What's on your mind?"

Crow looks from me to Jackyl and back again. "What does he know that I don't?" he demands.

"C'mon, J," Jackyl prods. "Tell us all about it."

I heave a sigh. "Nothing's wrong. I just…"

"Aw, fuck," Crow mutters.

"What?"

"You've fallen, and you can't get up."

Jackyl howls with laughter. "Good one, Pres."

Either I'm an idiot, or it wasn't that good. "What the hell's that supposed to mean?"

Crow smirks. "All I'm sayin' is I've seen that look before. And man are things about to get interesting."

Without another word, he turns to walk away. I spin around, but Jackyl's sauntering toward the hotel elevator, and there are too many people around for me to yell at him.

"Fuckers," I mutter, picking up my bag and hoisting it over my shoulder.

We're stuck in this hotel for the rest of the week, but the conference doesn't start until tomorrow, so I head to my room on the fourth floor to shower off the grime from the road.

Crow and Addi are going out for dinner tonight, which means the rest of us on this trip have time to play. Normally, I'd be all about hitting the local bars, but I'd be shit company right now, and I know it.

Damn woman messing up my head.

As soon as the elevator door closes behind me, I breathe a sigh of relief. At least I can lose my mind in peace.

My phone vibrates in my pocket, and for a split-second, my mood lifts thinking it's Wren, but then I remember that we didn't exchange numbers. Hell, I didn't even get her last name. I waited until she was sound asleep to slip out because I wanted to avoid any awkwardness. I don't do morning afters, but something tells me I should've made an exception.

I pull out my cell and glance at the screen, groaning when I see our road captain's name.

"What's up, Screamer?" I say.

"This is the biggest code blue I've ever seen," he grumbles. "Crow's gonna owe us big for forcing us around this many cops."

I stifle my laugh as I slip the key card in the slot when I reach my room. I agree with him, but as VP, I have to back our president. "Crow won't owe us shit. We protect our own, and Addi is one of us now."

"Yeah, yeah."

"Did you need something, or did you just call to bitch?"

"Both. Figured I'd get the bitchin' outta the way, though."

Chuckling, I flop down on the bed. "Thanks for that, I guess. Now, what—"

"I had to make some changes to our route home and wanted to run them by you."

"What's wrong with the original plan?"

"Don't tell me you missed all those construction signs warning about upcoming work," he says. "I don't know about you, but I'd like to avoid that mess if possible."

"Makes sense. Shoot me a screenshot of the new route you found, and I'll let you know if it's greenlit."

"Thanks, brother. I know I could've called Crow, but he and Addi just left, and I figure they want to be left alone."

"You figure right," I say with a laugh. "Anything else?"

"Nah. I'll get that over to you as soon as we disconnect."

After ending the call, I get to my feet and carry my bag into the bathroom. I'm just stepping into the shower when my cell pings with a text notification. I know Screamer can be a bit impatient, so I quickly wash my hair and body.

When I step out of the shower, I wrap a towel around my waist before picking up my phone to look over the new route. Everything appears in order, and I tap out a quick text.

> Me: Route is greenlit

> Screamer: Thx bro

Once I'm dressed in a pair of sweats, I pull up the room service menu on my cell. Deciding on steak and a loaded baked potato, I place my order and turn on the TV to find something to watch. Settling on a Dateline marathon, I kick back on the bed and tap on the Facebook icon on my phone.

I type 'Wren' into the search bar, and numerous results appear. Scrolling through them, my stomach tightens with anticipation, but when I don't see any picture I recognize, frustration settles in its place.

I've gotta find a way to get this chick out of my head before the conference starts tomorrow, or I'm gonna be useless to my club.

CHAPTER 4
WREN

I met someone.

"How was the drive here?"

I toss my purse onto the corner of the couch and sit facing Dr. Young, my therapist. She asks me the same question every session, but I suppose it's a good ice breaker considering I drive an hour to Austin every week to meet with her.

"It was fine. Construction's picking up," I tell her. "Fortunately, I won't hit rush hour traffic on the way back."

"Good." Dr. Young smiles. "So, anything exciting happen since we last met?"

Heat burns my cheek as I think about my night with Journey. "I met some—" I clamp my mouth shut as I shoot to my feet and begin to pace. "You're never gonna believe it, Doc."

Dr. Young's expression turns serious. "Aaron?"

"Who else would it be?" I snap, cracking my knuckles with each step I take.

"Why did you send Wren away?" she asks me.

"Because she was about to go all goo goo ga ga over a dude that needs his ass kicked from here to Timbuktu," I snarl. Rage boils my blood. "I swear, if I ever see him, he's toast."

"Did he hurt her?" Dr. Young asks.

Leave it to a woman to ask a ridiculous fucking question. "Of course, he hurt her. I wouldn't be here if he hadn't."

"Okay," she says calmly. "Why don't you sit down, and we can talk about what happened and why you feel like Wren needs you to protect her from him?"

I stare at her, scowling. "You know I don't sit. Fuck, Doc, you'd think you'd remember that after all these years."

"And you know I'll keep trying," she counters.

"Can we get back to our session?" I bark. "I've got shit to do."

"Sure." Dr. Young leans back in her chair. "So, tell me about the man who hurt Wren."

"He's a biker douchebag," I snarl. "A real wham bam, thank you, ma'am kinda prick."

"Ah," she says as if I just unlocked all the mysteries of the universe. "Now it's making sense."

"'Bout time," I grumble.

"So, Wren had a one-night stand, and you're upset because you think she wants more than that."

"I know she does. Me and the others have had to hear about it for days."

"Aaron, are you angry at the guy because he left her wanting more, or are you angry at Wren because you want her for yourself?"

Without thinking, I lunge toward Dr. Young and wrap my hand around her throat.

How dare she accuse me of being jealous.

Her eyes widen with fear, but she quickly masks it and gently rests her hand on my forearm. Our gazes lock, and for a moment, I pray for the life to drain out of her. My mind spirals, and I blink rapidly.

"Oh my heavens." I drop my hand and tears well in my eyes. "Dr. Young, I am so sorry. I tried to stop him sooner, but you know how he gets."

"I do… Peg."

"I can assure you, Aaron will be dealt with."

"I appreciate that, Peg, but you don't need to punish him."

"You know I can't ignore such blatantly violent

behavior," I explain. "Aaron may be a grown man, but I swear, sometimes he acts like a super-sized child throwing temper tantrums."

Dr. Young chuckles as she rubs her throat. The marks from where Aaron tried to choke her are slowly disappearing, but my disappointment in him isn't.

"Let me ask you, Peg," Dr. Young begins. "How do you feel about the man Wren met?"

"He's no good for our Wren," I say matter-of-factly. "No good at all."

"Why do you say that?"

"For heaven's sake, he's in a biker gang!"

"And that means he's not a good man?"

"It means he's a scoundrel."

"Is that how the others feel as well?"

I wave my hand dismissively and sit down on the couch across from the therapist. "You know how they are. Vixen wants to try him out for herself, and Rose thinks Wren needs to be more careful with her body. Kirby and Annie are too young to be subjected to such things, so they plug their ears to avoid hearing anything about it. And Mavis is blissfully unaware of the entire event because she checks out whenever a man is involved."

"Is Wren planning on seeing this man again?"

Not if I have anything to say about it.

"If she'd bothered to get his phone number, she probably would. Fortunately, she didn't."

"Fortunate for who? Wren? Or you?"

"I don't like what you're suggesting, Dr. Young."

"What is it you think I'm suggesting, Peg?"

"That I'm selfish. That we all are. That our existence to protect Wren is somehow tainted by ulterior motives."

"I'm sorry you feel that way. I was merely trying to determine why you all are so adamant that Wren still needs your protection. It's been years since her trauma, and she's a smart, capable woman."

Indignation wraps around me like a cold hug. "If you think we're just going to abandon her, you're not the competent therapist I thought you were." Shifting on the sofa, I stare at her diploma that's hanging on the wall.

"Peg, we've talked about this. I want to help Wren as much as you, but insulting me isn't how we accomplish that. Now, can you please get Wren for me? I'd really like to talk to her."

Returning my focus to Dr. Young, I stare at her for several long moments as if I can ascertain any hidden agenda. Her face begins to blur, and my body relaxes.

"Wren?" Dr. Young asks.

I shake my head to clear it. "What were we talking about? I, um, don't remember."

Dr. Young smiles reassuringly. "I asked you if anything exciting happened since our last session."

I grin at the memory of my night with Journey and nod. "Yeah."

"Care to tell me what it was?"

"I met someone."

CHAPTER 5
JOURNEY

I'm stubborn and won't stop.

"P-p-please don't k-kill me."

I glance at Poker, the club's enforcer, and the excitement on his face rivals my own. We've had Niles, a piece of shit gun for hire, in the Nightmare Room for a few hours now, but he has yet to tell us what we want to hear.

"Oh, we're not gonna kill you," I tell him. "Yet."

"Shit, maybe we'll spare your life completely," Poker adds. "But first, tell us who hired you."

"I already tol—"

My knuckles burn as I deliver another blow to his face. "And we obviously don't believe you," I snap.

"But I'm telling the truth," Niles insists. "It was all anonymous."

The fact of the matter is, he *is* being honest, which is odd for such a slimeball. But being honest isn't going to earn him any points with the Soulless Kings. He tried to run a few of us off the road on our return trip from the conference, and for that alone, he's a dead man walking.

Unfortunately for Niles, my brothers and I like to play with our prey before destroying them. It's so much fun to watch them squirm.

"Journey, I think we're gonna have to step it up a notch," Poker says, his tone full of anticipation.

I grin at him. "Blowtorch or cattle prod?"

"Why not both?" he counters.

"I like the way you think."

"Y-you're insane," Niles cries. "I can't t-tell you what I don't know."

While Poker gets the tools from the wall, I crouch down in front of Niles. "Here's the thing, motherfucker… You don't mess with SKMC and get away with it."

"No one was hurt," he says. "Can't you just let me off with a warning or something?"

I throw my head back and laugh. "A warning?" Glancing over my shoulder, I smirk at Poker. "Did you hear that, bro? He wants us to give him a warning like he's some kindergartner who made a mess with the finger paints."

"I heard," Poker says and walks toward us as he's turning on the blowtorch. He stops next to me and holds the flame inches from Niles' hand, which is secured to the chair he's sitting in. "How's this for a warning?" He shifts the flame, and the smell of burning flesh permeates the air.

Niles screams like the little bitch he is, but he remains conscious. I guess his balls are slightly bigger than I thought.

I straighten to my full height and take a few steps away from the two of them before crossing my arms over my chest. "Who hired you?" I ask, but Niles only shakes his head, so I nod at Poker. "Again."

Poker scorches his other hand, and the screams intensify.

"This is gonna keep happening until you talk," I remind Niles.

"Maybe he needs a little more incentive," Poker suggests, switching the cattle prod to his dominant hand. He presses the prongs to Niles' inner thigh, and seconds later, our captive jolts with a scream. "How 'bout now?"

This goes on for another five minutes before Niles passes out from the pain. Or maybe it's damage to his heart from all the shocks. Either way, when he's not screaming, the torture isn't nearly as fun.

"Now what?" Poker asks me.

I pull my cell out of my back pocket and glance at the time. "End it," I order. "We didn't need anything from him anyway, and I've got somewhere to be."

Poker groans. "Please don't tell me you're going to that bar again."

"Fine. I won't tell you."

I stride across the room and flatten my palm against the sensor so the door slides open.

"Dude, let it go," Poker advises from behind me. "No pussy is wor…"

His voice fades as the door closes, and I move down the hall to the stairs that lead to the main level of the clubhouse. I need a shower and a game plan before I head out.

Poker's not the only brother to give me a hard time about my search for Wren. When I asked Tracer for help, he laughed at me for a solid minute before I punched him in the jaw and demanded he put his tech skills to use. Since I had a first name and an address, it didn't take Tracer long to track the woman down… Wren Abbott.

Wren has plagued my thoughts and stared in my dreams for two weeks straight. I went back to her apartment a few times because I had to see her, but she was never home. I've also been back to the bar where we met, and nothing there either.

But I'm stubborn and won't stop. I need to see her

again, to figure out if our one night together was a fluke or something to be repeated. Problem is, I don't know which I prefer. I've never seen myself as the relationship type, but something about Wren isn't letting me move on.

"Yo, Journey!"

I veer to the left at Ghost's shout. "What's up?" I ask when I reach his side.

"Wanna wingman tonight?"

Narrowing my eyes at him, I ponder his question. I might trust him with my life, but I'm not as confident in his ability to not be a dick.

"Under one condition," I finally reply.

"What?"

"One joke or punchline at my expense, and I get to take it out on you in the Nightmare Room."

He chuckles, but there's more trepidation than humor in the sound. "Deal."

"Be ready to ride in thirty."

CHAPTER 6
WREN

No fuss, no muss.

Two months later...

"The latest sketches are perfect."

Rolling my eyes, I tuck my cell between my ear and shoulder as I lock the apartment door. Laura is Wren's agent, and sometimes I have to take these calls and pretend I'm her. I don't know if the other alters get stuck doing this shit, but I don't complain because I don't have to actually do any work. I'm all fun, all the time.

Take this evening for example... I'm only here because Wren couldn't cope with the stress piling on her. She's weak when it comes to matters regarding her childhood, and I step in to make it better.

"Glad to hear it," I reply, forcing as much sincerity into my tone as possible.

"The author is hoping you can have the final artwork submitted by the end of the month," Laura says. "Is that doable?"

I pause for a moment, pretending to be checking a schedule before responding. "Yep. I can do that."

Between Wren and Drew, it shouldn't be a problem.

"Perfect," she gushes. "I'll eagerly wait for the files."

Laura rambles for a few more minutes, and I pretend to listen. As soon as we end the call, I toss the phone onto the passenger seat of the car and glance into the backseat to make sure it's not as messy as the last time I used it. I don't know who keeps driving, but they don't know how to deal with trash one iota.

It doesn't take long before I'm parking on a side street near a bar I like to go to on Fridays because that's when they have their ladies' night. It's a perfect storm for finding a casual hookup.

As soon as I step inside, music fills my ears, and I push away all thoughts of anything beyond having a good time.

"Mavis!"

I whirl to my right at the sound of my name and grin when I see Lydia standing at the end of the bar.

She and I have shared some crazy nights together, and a repeat performance might be exactly what I need.

Closing the distance between us, I contemplate all the wicked things I'm going to do to her later. When I'm within reach, she grabs the front of my shirt and yanks me in for a kiss. I can taste the cranberry and lime from her Cosmopolitan, and the combination of that and her is delicious.

"I haven't seen you in a while," Lydia says when I break contact. "Where the hell have you been?"

"Here, there, everywhere."

She laughs at that, and the sound is even more intoxicating than her taste. "Well, I've missed you."

Red flags flash in front of my face like giant hazard warnings. Lydia is amazing, but I don't do commitment of any kind. I can't.

"I'm here now," I say.

She lowers her gaze to my cleavage and runs a finger from my collarbone to between my tits. "Thank God," she whispers. "The things I wanna do to you…"

"How about we take this to your place?"

She takes a few twenties out of her purse and tosses them onto the bar before wrapping an arm around my shoulders and steering me toward the door. Just as I reach out to push it open, it swings outward, and a large man in jeans and a leather vest blocks my path.

"Wren?"

I try to step around him, but there's not enough room. "Excuse me."

"Seriously?" he scoffs. "You're not even gonna say hi?"

"Why would I?"

"Jesus, Wren, that's cold."

"Mavis, who is this guy?" Lydia asks.

"Mavis?" he repeats. "You told me your name was Wren."

And this is why Peg bitches when I ignore Wren's private life.

"I've never seen you before in my life," I insist. "Now, if you'll ex—"

"Never seen me before?" he says, heat lacing his tone. "The name's Journey, and you saw every fucking inch of me two months ago. Not to mention, I saw, felt, *and* tasted every inch of you."

"Apparently, that was a chick named Wren," I counter pointedly. "I'm not her. My name is Mavis, and I'm into pussies, not dicks."

"If what I'm saying isn't true, then how would I know that you've got a birthmark shaped like a horseshoe on your right ass cheek?"

I link my fingers with Lydia's and push past him.

"Fuck off," I snap as soon as the night air hits my skin.

Journey sputters a retort, but I can't make out any more than the words 'bitch', 'mental case', and 'punked'. Not that it matters what he says. He didn't look the least bit familiar to me, but he clearly knows Wren.

"Mavis, would you stop?" Lydia says as she comes to a halt when we reach the end of the block.

I face her. "What?"

"What?" she repeats. "*You* tell *me* what. Who was that?"

Shrugging, I force a smile. "Said his name was Journey."

"Yeah, okay, I heard that, too. But he clearly knows you." She frowns. "I mean, he knew about your birthmark."

"C'mon, Lydia," I prod. "I can't be the only chick in the world to have a birthmark on her ass cheek."

Her shoulders slump, and she seems to ponder that line of thinking. She must accept it because she leans forward and nibbles on my bottom lip.

"See, this is what I had in mind," I tease when she pulls back. "You, me, no clothes, and raging hormones."

Lydia's lips tilt into a full-blown smile. "Then let's go."

I follow her to her car, knowing she'll bring me back to mine when the fun is over. That's our routine. No fuss, no muss.

Four hours and plenty of orgasms later, I'm on my way back to the apartment. By the time I crawl under the covers, I'm fully aware that once tonight becomes common knowledge among the others, it'll be quite a while before Peg lets me out to play again.

CHAPTER 7
JOURNEY

She could be with them for all I know.

"This shit is getting outta control."

I nod at Crow before glancing around the table at my brothers' expressions, and each of them mirror my own. Pres called church on an emergency basis, and when that happens, nothing good ever comes of it. This time is proving to be no exception.

"It's been relatively quiet since we took out Niles," I chime in. "I was hoping that'd be the end of it."

"It seemed like it was," Crow says. "But apparently, all we did was piss off the top dog who's been biding his time and planning the club's demise."

"And Addi's sure about the intel?" Ghost asks.

Crow scowls. "As sure as she can be."

"I dug into it a little before church," Tracer says. "So far, all the info she's provided can be corroborated."

"So, we're fucked," Python bites out from his seat at the other end of the long table.

Crow's eyes darken. "We're Soulless Kings. We're never fucked."

"Uh, Pres," Fudge begins. "I'm pretty sure the fact that another MC is moving on our territory and managing to recruit people who want us dead is the very definition of fucked."

Pres pounds the table with his fist, and drinks slosh over the rim of their cups. "We've been down this road before and come out better for it. It'll be the same this time."

"I gotta say, I'm disappointed in the doubt I'm hearing," I add. "Soulless Kings don't back down, and we never lose. Either get on board with that or get the fuck out."

Crow straightens, shifting his stare from one brother to the next as if daring them to leave. Everyone remains seated, and after a few tense moments, Crow's shoulder's relax.

"Good. Now instead of giving in like pussies, let's figure this shit out so we can put a stop to it."

"I think the first step is learning everything we

can about the Wingless Angels MC," Screamer states. "Know thy enemy and all that bullshit."

"I had Tracer email you all a copy of what Addi was able to pull together from a law enforcement perspective, and I've reached out to Shuffle with Limitless Throttle MC for more info," Crow informs us. "But here are the bullet points: Drugs, prostitution, and wreaking as much havoc as humanly possible."

"So, real choir boys then?" Poker comments dryly.

"We're not saints," Crow says. "But we sure as fuck ain't as bad as them. Tracer, fill 'em in what you've found so far."

"I cross-referenced arrest records with hospital records, and I also started sifting through social media. Basically, it amounts to dozens of arrests, broken bones, branding, tainted drugs, and a whole lot of fear. These guys don't fuck around, and their president, Stone, is the worst of them. He's serving a life sentence for a double murder, and he still manages to run his club with an iron fist. And the members are loyal to a fault."

"Wait a sec," Ghost demands. "Are you seriously telling us that he runs his entire club from prison?"

Tracer nods.

"This is a whole new level we're playing at,"

Screamer says. "It's not like we can get to the head of the snake to chop it off."

"Maybe not," Crow admits. "But there are other ways to kill a snake."

"We go for every single weak spot below the head," I add.

"Exactly." Crow sits for the first time since we all entered the room. "We take the time we need to learn all we can, to plan, and then we strike. And Shuffle has pledged his club as backup if we want it."

"And in the meantime, Wingless Angels encroach on our territory?" Python snaps. "I don't think so."

"For now, we operate as usual. We deal with things as they come. If we catch them working on our turf, we handle it. We do what we do in any of those situations. Keep your eyes and ears open at all times because I have no clue when, where, or how they will strike. But we don't let it be known that we're aware of who they are and their hatred for us." Crow inhales deeply. "Fuck, I don't even know why Stone has it out for us. But we'll figure it out, and when we do, we take them down."

"Why do I get the feeling that life is about to get infinitely more complicated?" Jackyl asks, speaking for the first time.

I frown. "Because it is."

"Any questions?" Crow asks. When no one speaks up, he nods. "Dismissed."

One by one, my brothers file out of the room, but Tracer hangs back. Before church assembled, I told him I needed a favor, and it's now or never.

"How'd it go with Wren?" he asks as soon as we're the only two left.

"I don't even know how to answer that," I admit. "It was… odd."

"Odd?"

"She acted like she didn't even know me," I tell him. "And she was fucking convincing, bro. Something about that chick is off, and I need to know what. Especially now that we've got this new threat. She could be with them for all I know."

"So you want me to dig?"

"As deep as you fucking can."

CHAPTER 8
WREN

Might as well get used to being alone.

"Press one to accept this call."

I stare at the screen, wondering what the hell I was thinking when I answered the call. I've managed to avoid most contact with my father since his trial, and I'd be smart to keep it that way.

Then why'd you fucking answer?

Instead of pressing one, I disconnect the call and drop my phone onto the coffee table like I'm playing a game of Hot Potato and the song has ended. My heart thumps in my chest, and my hands become clammy.

"No," I whisper. "No, no, no."

My vision blurs, and the voices in my head get louder. I know what that means, and I have to stop it. Leah's coming over, and the last time an alter was fronting around a friend, I became a laughing stock.

I spent years not understanding why I'd lose time and why people would treat me with familiarity when I had no clue who they were. Moving from one foster home to another because the parents were afraid of me didn't help either.

Broken, fractured, crazy… You name it, I've likely been called it.

Then I aged out of the system and found Dr. Young. She put a name to what was happening to me: Dissociative Identity Disorder. Apparently, watching my dad bludgeon my mom and brother to death was so traumatic that my mind splintered into different personalities in order to protect itself.

Dr. Young gave me hope when I needed it the most. Without her, I'd probably be six feet under. I wouldn't say that life is easy by any stretch of the imagination, but she's helped me understand what's going on and taught me ways to process stressful situations to reduce the risk of switching.

I breathe in and out slowly, counting to seven with every inhale and exhale. Soon, my vision clears, and I'm completely myself again. The voices are still there, but they're quieter, calmer.

Thirteen.

That's the number of people living rent-free in my head.

Thirteen different personalities, each one keeping me safe from one thing or another.

Thirteen alters who take control of my body when they perceive a threat.

I wish I knew them, understood them, could regulate them. I'm trying. Therapy and medication help, but I don't think it's something that will ever completely go away. Which means lost time, amnesia, and a host of other problems that can arise, all because of being dealt a shitty hand in the father department.

A knock on the door startles me, reminding me I have plans for tonight. It'd probably be smart to cancel, considering the stress of my dad trying to reach out, but fuck it.

Leah frowns when I open the door and she sees what I'm wearing. I glance down and take in my leggings and flimsy old t-shirt before smiling lopsided at her.

"I'm changing," I assure her.

"Thank God." Leah comes in when I step aside. "I mean, you look adorable, but I don't think that's the vibe you want to project during a night on the town."

"Definitely not."

Ten minutes later, we're walking out the door, and

I'm dressed in tight jeans, black strappy sandals, and a cobalt blue tank. We take my car since I don't drink as much as Leah due to my *issues*, and she talks nonstop on the way to the bar.

"I wonder if he'll be here again," she muses as I park.

"Who?"

"Have you been listening at all?" she demands with a huff of laughter. "That biker guy."

"Journey?"

"No, the other one," she says. "Jackyl."

"Oh."

As we walk inside, she throws an arm around my shoulders and pulls me close. "You really liked that guy, didn't you?"

"Jackyl?"

"No, Journey." We reach the bar, and she lifts her hand to get the bartender's attention. "Can I get a gin and tonic?"

"And you?" the bartender asks me.

"Just a Coke, please." Leah gives me a look, and I shrug. "I'm driving."

The truth is, there's too much going on in my head tonight to risk consuming any alcohol. The last thing I wanna do is trigger a switch here.

"You can have at least one," she counters.

"I'm good. Really."

"Suit yourself."

As soon as we have our drinks, we make our way to a high-top table that gives us the best view of the door. Not two minutes pass, and it swings open.

"He's here!" she exclaims, but then her expression falls. "But it looks like he's alone."

Jackyl steps inside, letting the door slam closed behind him. Any hope that Journey would be with him vanishes. The biker scans the crowd, and when his eyes land on us, he grins.

He strides across the room, pulling his cell out of his pocket as he walks. He appears to type a text before putting it away.

"Fancy meeting you ladies here," he says when he's within earshot.

Leah bats her eyelashes, shamelessly flirting without a single word. Jackyl takes her glass from her and sets it on the table. Then he grabs her hand and practically drags her onto the dance floor.

"Yeah, uh, I'll just wait here," I mumble to no one in particular.

Might as well get used to being alone.

CHAPTER 9
JOURNEY

It is her.

"Where are you headed in such a hurry?"

I skid to a stop and turn to face Ghost. Jackyl just texted me that Wren's at the bar tonight, and I've got questions… lots of fucking questions.

"Out."

"No shit, Sherlock," Ghost counters. "Any place in particular?"

"Nope."

"Ah, so Ballinger's again?"

"Nope."

He grins mischievously. "Have fun then."

"Bite me," I snap before whirling around and racing out of the clubhouse.

I throw my leg over my Harley and start her up.

The rumble of the machine lulls me into a false sense of security, and I use the ride to replay my last conversation with Tracer in my mind.

"Dude, you were right."

I close the door to Tracer's room and move to stand behind him. He's been digging into Wren for me, trying to make sense of my second encounter with her.

"About?" I ask, not at all sure I want to know what he's found.

"That chick is crazy with a capital 'C'."

I groan. "How so?"

"Let's just say, life with her would never be dull."

"How. So?"

"You might wanna sit down," he suggests, nodding toward the lounge chair he has in the corner. "There's a lot of information to digest."

I hesitate for a moment before moving to the chair, sitting, and throwing my legs over the arm. "Okay. Hit me."

"For starters, she's squeaky clean as far as a criminal record, so that's good."

"Because I'd give a damn if she had a record."

"Fair enough. But at least it's less likely that she's in cahoots with any enemies of the club."

"Yeah, yeah, that's good."

"Now onto the not-so-good." Tracer takes a deep

breath. "She grew up in foster care, bouncing from one fam—"

"So her parents were pieces of shit," I snap, inexplicably angry on Wren's behalf.

"Well…"

I level my stare on him. "Well, what?"

"Her father is a piece of shit. Worse than that, actually." His eyes harden. "He killed her mom and baby brother."

"Jesus Christ," I mutter. "When?"

"From all accounts, Wren was five and present when it happened. Fucker used a hammer as a weapon."

"Please tell me he's dead," I snarl.

"'Fraid not," he says. "Serving a life sentence, though."

"Not good enough."

"No, it's not, but that's the justice system for ya."

Shaking my head, I try to process what he's told me so far. Just when I think I've seen the worst of humanity, humanity decides to pop back for an encore.

"Okay, Wren had a worse than shitty childhood," I say. "But that still doesn't explain her behavior at Ballinger's."

"I'm getting to that," Tracer informs me.

"Fuck, there's more?"

He chuckles, but there's no humor in it. "Oh yeah."

Shoving a hand through my hair, I swing my feet to

the floor and lean forward. "What else could there possibly be?"

Tracer glances at his computer and taps his mouse a few times before his printer starts spitting out papers. It takes a few minutes for everything to print, and he watches me warily as it does.

"Here," he says as he hands me a stack. "I think you should read these on your own."

Taking the pages of information, I maintain eye contact with him, almost as if looking at the words will suck me into another dimension.

Parking in the lot across the street from Ballinger's, my brain locks onto the one line in the massive amount of mental health jargon I read about Wren: Patient has been diagnosed with Dissociative Identity Disorder, and the presence of thirteen alters have been observed.

Music filters out through the open door of the bar, and I let it overtake my thoughts. When I step inside, I immediately seek out Wren. It doesn't take more than a few seconds for my eyes to land on her, and she's standing at the bar with her friend, Leah, and Jackyl.

As if we're connected by an invisible tether, Wren's gaze shifts, and her eyes widen. I assume that means it's really her because there's recognition in her expression.

I cross the room, weaving my way through small groups of people, and when I reach her, I smile. Finally registering my presence, Jackyl glances at me and opens his mouth to say something, but Wren beats him to the punch.

"Journey."

Relief floods my system.

It is her.

"Hi, Wren."

CHAPTER 10
WREN

Right now, under his scrutiny, fear becomes real.

"It is Wren, right?"

Leah elbows me in the side, stunning me out of my stupor. It's been a while since I saw Journey, and I was beginning to think I imagined the entire night with him.

"Yep. Wren."

Journey grins devilishly. "I don't remember you being this… shy."

"I'm surprised you remember me at all," I counter, my tone harsher than I intend.

His grin slips, but only for a moment. "Really? Because last time we ran into each other, you drew a complete blank when it came to me."

Last time we ran into each other?

"I'm sure you're mistaken." I glance at Leah. "We should go."

"But I just got here," Journey says, a pleading quality to his words, as he reaches for my hand.

When his fingers brush mine, a jolt of electricity zaps every single one of my nerve endings, and I have to tense my muscles to keep from collapsing into a puddle of rampant hormones on the floor.

"Yeah, Wren," Leah adds. "He just got here."

I roll my eyes at my friend. She knows why I'm hesitant to have a repeat performance with Journey, but she also *doesn't* know when to quit. We have one of those love/hate friendships.

"I'm sorry," I say, surprised at the genuine regret in my words. "I have to go."

I push past Journey, ignoring Leah's pleas that I stay, and rush to leave the bar. When I reach my car, I release the breath I didn't even realize I was holding. Guilt tries to rear its ugly head at leaving my friend behind, but I remind myself that Leah's resourceful and will find a way home safely.

As soon as I start the car, my cell rings. I pull it from my purse and glance at the screen. Leah's name flashes, but I ignore the call. Instead, I send her a quick text.

> Me: I'm okay. I'll pay for your Uber. Have fun tonight.

I don't wait for her reply before tossing my phone onto the passenger seat and putting the car in gear to pull away from the curb. By the time I reach my apartment complex, my mind is spiraling, and the voices are intensifying.

Forget about him. It'd just end in heartache.

C'mon, have some fun. Live a little.

Good girl, Wren. You're better than cavorting with strange men.

Journey's big and scary.

I'd mount that horse and ride him into the sunset any time.

"Shut up," I mutter as I unlock my front door and stride inside. "Shut up, shut up, shut up!"

As soon as I'm locked inside, I quickly make my way to my bedroom, stripping as I go. When the voices get this loud, I start to get uncomfortable in my own clothes, my own skin.

Naked, I climb into bed and pull the covers over my head in an effort to shut the world out. It doesn't make the voices go away, but it does quiet them a little.

I spend a few minutes breathing in and out, in and out, trying to calm my mind. When that stops working, I start counting to one hundred. Dr. Young has taught me so many tips and tricks to keep my anxiety and the voices to a minimum, but they don't always work.

Thirty-six, thirty-seven, thirty-eight, thirty-nine, forty, fort—

Thud, thud, thud.

Shoving the blankets off of me, I sit up straight and glare at the ceiling.

Why, God? Why is someone pounding on my door now?

Don't answer it. Nothing good happens after a late-night knock on a door.

Aw, c'mon, answer it. Maybe it's him!

I'll fuckin' kill him.

So much for a calm mind.

I scramble off the bed to rifle through my dresser for a pair of shorts and a t-shirt. Once I'm as decent as I'm gonna get, I walk to the door.

"I'm coming," I shout, annoyed at the continued pounding. "Don't get your panties in a wad."

After flipping the lock, I yank open the door. My mouth goes bone-dry when I see Journey standing at the threshold, his hand up as if he was getting ready to knock again.

"What do you want?" I demand, crossing my arms over my chest and blocking the entrance.

"Wren?"

"Who the hell else would it be?" I counter, my hackles rising.

Journey stares at me as if I've grown two heads, and unease begins to trickle in. He didn't scare me when we initially met. Hell, I brought him home after only a few minutes in his company. But right now, under his current scrutiny, fear becomes real.

"You tell me," he says quietly.

The panic coursing through my veins catapults me back in time, and I run to duck behind the couch.

"Wren?" the man calls out. "What the hell are you doing?"

Who's Wren?

"My Daddy will hurt you," I say, my voice small and wobbly.

Footsteps thud on the floor, and I curl into a ball as they get closer.

"Your Daddy?" he asks.

I nod frantically but don't speak because my voice is stuck in my throat. Squeezing my eyes shut, I try to swallow so I can make words come out.

"He's scary, mister," I croak. "Please, just go."

"Wren, please," he replies. "Come out of there and talk to me."

"I'm not Wren!" I yell. "She left because she was scared."

"She left?"

"Mister, please," I plead. "Leave me alone."

"Okay, okay. But…"

"He's coming," I tell him, hearing the sounds that warn me that Daddy's home. "Don't tell him where I'm at."

"I won't." The man moves into my line of sight and smiles, but my fear isn't eased. "Can you tell me your name before I go?"

I think about it for a moment and decide that it might be a good thing if someone else knows about me. If anything bad happens, maybe he can get help.

"Annie. My name's Annie."

CHAPTER 11
JOURNEY

This woman got her hooks into me from the moment I laid eyes on her.

"My name's Annie."

I stare at the woman curled up in the fetal position behind the couch. Her beautiful eyes swim with unshed tears, and her body trembles. I know she's a grown-up, but she's acting very much like a small child.

"Annie, I'm Journey," I say carefully.

I remember reading about Annie in the notes from Wren's therapist. Based on Dr. Young's observations, Annie is approximately five years old, the same age Wren was when her piece-of-shit father killed her family.

"You have to leave," she says, her bottom lip quivering. "I don't want you to get hurt."

"Why would I get hurt?" I ask.

Her gaze drops to my chest, and I glance down to see what she's looking at. A second later, she stretches a hand and points at the patches on my cut.

"He hurts people that make him mad. And you'll make him mad."

What?

"I'm not gonna let him hurt me." I hesitantly wrap my hand around hers, fully expecting her to pull away. Shock hammers in my chest when she doesn't. "I won't let him hurt you, either."

Wren's—or is it Annie's?—eyes widen. "You won't?" she asks.

"I'll never let anything happen to you. I promise."

The words resonate deep in my soul, and I realize how much I mean them. This woman got her hooks into me from the moment I laid eyes on her, and those hooks have only dug themselves deeper the more I've learned about her.

I just wish I learned it all from her and not reports Tracer dug up.

My president's words roll around in my head.

"Aw, fuck," Crow mutters.

"What?"

"You've fallen, and you can't get up."

"What the hell's that supposed to mean?"

Crow smirks. "All I'm sayin' is I've seen that look before. And man, are things about to get interesting."

"My mommy says you shouldn't make promises."

The tiny voice coming from Wren's mouth snaps me back to the present.

"Why's that?"

"Because promises can be broken, and breaking a promise is lying, and lying is bad."

I smile at her. "You're right. Lying is bad. So, it's a good thing I'm not a liar." I squeeze her hand reassuringly. "Do you think you can come out from behind the couch for me?"

Slowly, she uncurls her body, each muscle seeming to visibly relax one by one. "Are you sure he's not here?"

"Who?" I ask, knowing exactly who she's referring to but needing to hear her say it again.

"Daddy," she whispers.

I make a show of glancing over my shoulder and around the room before returning my attention to her. "He's not here, Annie. It's just you and me."

And Wren.

After a few moments, she nods and uses my hand for leverage to pull herself up. Even at her full grown height, she's small compared to me. The top of her head is level with my shoulders, and without thinking, I pull her close and tuck her under my chin.

She shudders as if letting go of all her apprehension. "You're warm," she says against my shirt.

I chuckle. Having her this close is pure torture, but I remind myself, and my cock, that now is not the time.

"Are you cold?" I ask.

"A little." As soon as the words leave her mouth, she yawns loudly.

"Tired, too, huh?" She nods so I continue. "Why don't you let me tuck you into bed so you can get some sleep?"

"But then you'll leave," she says almost frantically. "And if you leave, he can get to me."

"I won't leave."

"Promise?"

"I thought promises were bad."

She shrugs. "You said you aren't a liar so I guess it's okay if you promise."

"Then yes, I promise I won't leave."

"Okay."

I lift her into my arms and carry her down the hallway until I reach an open door. A quick glance tells me it's her bedroom, and when my legs hit the mattress, I gently lay her down.

"Will you sit with me until I fall asleep?" she asks, rubbing her eyes with her fists.

Um…

"Sure."

As I crawl onto the bed next to her, she pulls the covers over herself, and I'm careful to stay above them. I should stand up and walk out immediately, but I can't bring myself to move. I made a promise, afterall.

Time seems to stand still as she tosses and turns, and before I know it, I doze off. And then I'm rudely awakened by a sharp elbow to my stomach.

"What the fuck are you doing here?"

I blink several times to clear the sleep from my eyes and turn to face Wren. Rage and confusion war in her expression, and when she raises her arm to elbow me again, I grab her hand mid-air.

"Hit me again, and there'll be consequences," I snarl, rattled by her behavior.

"Answer my question," she retorts as she swings her legs over the edge of the bed, yanking the blanket with her, and stands.

"You asked me to stay," I blurt. When her forehead wrinkles with confusion, I go on. "Well, you, but not you." I rub my hands over my face, trying to find the right words. "I think it was you when I got here, but then something happened. I, uh…"

"Fuck," she mutters harshly.

I hurry to my feet and face her. "Wren, it's okay, really. I, um, was happy to stay."

"Who asked you to stay?" she demands.

"What?"

She walks around the bed and comes to a stop a foot in front of me. "Who asked you to stay last night? You said it wasn't me, so who?"

"Annie."

Her entire body stiffens. "You need to leave."

"What?"

"Go," she snaps. "Get out of my apartment before I call the cops."

"Wait a damn minute," I bark. "Why the fuck would you ca—"

Wren's entire demeanor shifts from angry confusion to distraught. Her shoulders slump, and she twists to plop onto the mattress.

"Please, Journey," she says with sadness in her tone. "Please just go."

CHAPTER 12
WREN

No, thanks.

"Nothing happened, if that's wh—"

"Go!" I scream, willing my tears to remain unshed until I'm alone.

Despite my refusal to look him in the eye, I can feel him boring holes into me with his stare. Heat licks my skin, and I silently beg my traitorous body to calm the fuck down. Apparently, even when I'm pissed at and scared of this man, the effect he has on me is unparalleled to anything I've ever experienced.

"Wren, look at me," he says firmly. I shake my head vigorously, and he sighs. "Fine. I'll go, but this doesn't mean I'm giving up."

I open my mouth to argue with him, but his retreating footsteps force me to stay silent. My front door opens and closes, and for the first time since I woke up, my heart rate begins to slow.

Scrambling from the bed, I race to my living room to look out the window and catch a glimpse of Journey riding his Harley out of the parking lot. The warmth I felt earlier fades to a bitter cold, and I find myself wanting to run after him.

Crazy.

Rather than do something stupid, I head to the bathroom to take a hot shower. It doesn't matter how my body feels, or how a piece of me wants to let Journey in. Someone like me isn't built for relationships, and someone like him can't possibly take on the immense stress that comes from my disability.

I don't linger in the shower, knowing that I need to distract my mind. As soon as I'm done, I dry off and dress in comfortable clothes so I can work on my latest assignment.

Flipping the light on in the spare bedroom, I take in the small art studio I've created since moving in a few years ago. There was a time in my life that I resented the fact that I couldn't hold a normal job, but I'm at peace with how things are.

Or I had been until a certain biker barreled into my life.

Journey has remained on my mind since that first night with him, and I'd accepted the fact that all he'd ever be was a memory. But then I woke up this morning, and there he was.

When he said the name Annie, I knew he witnessed an aspect of my life that I don't share with just anyone. He's been a memory I couldn't shake, but now, he's woven a web around my soul, and I'm afraid of what that means.

Nope. Not going there.

I throw myself into my illustrations for the next several hours, only stopping when my stomach growls. I tend to forget that food is a necessity when I'm lost in my work.

Taking a break for sustenance, I grab my cell on the way to the kitchen so I can check my emails while I eat. I heat up some leftovers and carry it to the living room, where I sit on the couch and dig in.

When I tap my cell's screen, it comes to life, and I see that I've got a barrage of missed texts from Leah.

Shit.

> Leah: Just checking in on u after last night. Hope ur ok

> Leah: Wren, I've been patient, but ur leaving me on read and I'm worried

> Leah: Dammit, respond to me!

> Leah: If I don't hear from u soon, I'm coming over

Her last text came through twenty minutes ago, and I breathe a sigh of relief that she hasn't shown up yet. I switch to her contact info and hit the call button.

"Where the hell have you been?" she demands when she answers, worry clear in her tone.

"Sorry, I've been working. You know how I get sometimes."

She snorts. "Yeah, yeah, I do. But shit, Wren. After the way you left Ballinger's last night and the way Journey took off after you, I was freaking out."

"I'm fine, promise."

As soon as the words leave my mouth, a snippet of memory, something about promises, tries to surface, but I can't quite latch onto it.

"Great, you're fine," she snaps. "Now I need to get my blood pressure under control."

"Why? What's wrong?"

"You scared me!" she shrieks.

Guilt settles like a lead balloon in my stomach. "I really am sorry, Leah. Do you wanna come over and see for yourself that I'm okay?"

Leah snorts again. "No. Oh, trust me, I would if I could, but I've got stuff to get done before…"

"Before what?" I prod.

"I have a date tonight."

"Really? Who's the lucky guy?"

"Uh, Jackyl."

At the mention of the biker she's set her sights on, an image of Journey pops into my head.

"Hey, maybe you and Journey could double-date with us," she says when I remain silent.

"Yeah, that's not gonna happen."

"Why? You two clearly have chemistry."

"You know why."

"Wren, you can't spend your entire life alone because you're scared."

"I'm not alone," I remind her. "I've got you."

"You know what I mean."

"I do, and my answer is the same. I'm not seeing Journey again. There is nothing good that could come from it. I'd end up getting attached, and when he inevitably gets sick of my numerous personalities, he'll break my heart. No, thanks."

"And what if he doesn't get sick of you or them?" she counters.

But this doesn't mean I'm giving up.

Journey's words before he left echo in my skull, but I shake them away.

"That's not something I'm willing to wait and find out."

CHAPTER 13
JOURNEY

She might have been born from evil, but she doesn't have an ounce of bad in her.

"Sit down, and shut up!"

Crow glares at each brother as he swivels his gaze around the table. Today was supposed to be a day off from club business, but Pres called an emergency meeting, so here we are.

Once the chatter stops and my brothers sit down, Pres focuses his attention on me. "Something you wanna share with the class, J?"

I narrow my eyes at him. "What would I have to share?"

His stare moves from me to Tracer and back again.

Fuck.

Whipping my head to look at our resident techie and security guru, I cross my arms over my chest. "What the fuck, brother? You told him?"

To his credit, a flash of shame flickers in Tracer's eyes. "Not exactly something I could keep to myself."

"Care to fill the rest of us in?" Ghost asks.

Crow glances at me. "VP?"

I heave a sigh. "I assume this is all about Wren."

"The chick you've had a hard-on for?" Screamer asks.

"It's more than a hard-on," Jackyl adds. "Bro's a fuckin' goner."

"Shut the hell up," I snap before continuing. "I don't know why Wren is club business, but yeah, she's the woman I met at Ballinger's."

"She's club business because she just happened to walk into the picture around the same time as the Wingless Angels MC," Crow snarls.

"Yeah, so?"

"So, the bitch is unhinged," Crow says. "And I'm—"

I'm out of my chair and landing a blow to his face in a split second. My knuckles burn at the contact, but I welcome the sensation.

"She's not a bitch," I growl.

Crow levels his eyes on mine as he wiggles his jaw back and forth. "I'm gonna give you a pass for that punch since I saw the writing on the wall when it comes to Wren as soon as I learned of her existence. But hit me again, and you're gone. Got it?"

"That's a good deal if I've ever heard one," Fudge comments.

He's right, it is. I know I shouldn't have let my anger get the better of me, but when it comes to Wren, I'm not exactly operating on all cylinders. She's got me twisted in knots.

Finally, I nod as I clench my hands into fists. "Sorry, man. It's just…"

"Seriously?" Python barks. "First Crow, and now you?"

"What?" I demand.

"Don't get me wrong, Addi's great, but if you're all gonna start falling like dominos, I might have to get out," Python explains. "No need to get caught up in that trend."

"Jesus, I'm not making Wren my old lady," I grumble.

"Journey, you just punched Crow for calling her a bitch," Poker states matter-of-factly. "You can deny it all you want, but you've claimed her."

I think about his statement for a moment and

realize he's not wrong. When I left Wren's house this morning, I told her I wasn't giving up. And I'm not. So, yeah, I guess that makes her mine and mine alone.

"Consider her claimed," I say. "She's not a threat to the club, and now she's one of us, so if any of you have a fucking problem with that, see me after church, and we'll sort it out."

"As sweet as that is," Crow begins. "I'm not convinced that she's not a threat."

"I get that her showing up at the same time as Wingless Angels might not be a coincidence," Ghost begins. "But I can't get past the 'unhinged' comment. What the hell does that mean?"

Again, Crow stares at me as if waiting for me to fill in the blanks.

"Wren has some issues in her—"

Tracer snorts. "Issues is an understatement."

I scowl at him. "Since you like to run your mouth so much, why don't you explain?"

"Dude, what was I supposed to do?" Tracer counters. "It's not like multiple personalities gives a person a free pass on evil."

All eyes shift to me.

"Multiple personalities?" Fudge asks.

I sit back down and frown. "Yeah, multiple

personalities," I confirm. "She developed them when she witnessed her father bludgeon her mother and brother to death with a hammer. She might have been born from evil, but she doesn't have an ounce of bad in her."

"And you can be sure of this how?" Jackyl asks. "You barely know her."

"How can you be sure Leah isn't a threat?" I snap. "She was with Wren the night we met. Maybe she's who we should be discussing like she's a tabloid headline."

"Touché."

"Look, I might not know everything there is to know about Wren," I explain. "But you all trust me, right?" Each of them nods. "Then give me the benefit of the doubt by extending her the same courtesy." I glance at Crow. "Please?"

"Let's vote on it," Pres says. "Thump twice if you're in favor of giving Journey some leeway when it comes to Wren."

There's a beat of silence before, one by one, they thump their fists on the table twice. I release a breath I didn't even realize I was holding. Soulless Kings MC is my life, and I've never questioned my loyalty to it and vice versa. I'm beyond grateful that isn't changing today.

"I guess that settles that," Crow says. "But mark my words, if Wren's name pops in anything related to the Wingless Angels, we'll be putting her fate to another vote, mental health problems be damned."

"Understood."

"Good." Crow shoves a hand through his hair and sits at the head of the table for the first time since he walked into the room. "Now, the Wingless Angels… Any new info on them?"

"Not much," Tracer replies. "Besides what Addi's already told us, there's not much out there. Their president's identity seems to be a closely guarded secret. His road name, Stone, is the *only* thing I've been able to find."

"How is that possible?" Ghost asks. "If he's in prison, there's a record somewhere to tie the name Stone to a legal name."

"You'd think, wouldn't you?" Tracer says. "But I'm telling you, there's nothing. Stone and his MC must have friends in high places for that info to be buried as deep as it is."

"Has anyone been able to track down any of their members?" Crow asks.

"Just what Addi already told us," Poker chimes in. "Which, as you know, isn't a ton. We know what they do, we know what they call themselves, but finding them has proven more difficult."

"As of this minute, Wingless Angels are to be considered public enemy number one. We eat, sleep, breathe that club until we can take them down. If it were just a territory dispute, I could be persuaded to be patient, but they've already tried to run us off the road and made threats on our lives. They don't get to get away with that shit."

"I'm on board," I say. "And will do everything I can to bring them down, but I'm also going to keep watch over Wren. She's now linked with me and, therefore, the club. I won't let them get to her either."

"I figured," Crow admits. "You claimed her, so she's got the right to the same protection as Addi. But I'll remind yo—"

"One step out of line, and she's fucked," I snap. "Yeah, you made that clear."

"Good." He glances around the room. "Any questions?"

"Nope."

"Nadda."

"Don't think so."

"All good here."

My brothers all speak over one another before Crow nods.

"Church dismissed."

After they've all left the room and I'm alone, I lean back in my chair and stare at the ceiling. There isn't a single part of me that thinks Wren is anything other than pure light, but what if one of her personalities is? Can I extricate myself from her and hand her over to Crow, or will I have to cut ties with the only family I have?

Sonofabitch.

CHAPTER 14
WREN

YOU CAN RUN, BUT YOU CAN'T HIDE.

"I can't wait to deliver these."

I smile at Laura, who's been gushing over the final drawings I brought to her for the last twenty minutes. I've been so preoccupied lately with thoughts of Journey that I was starting to worry that I wouldn't finish them in time, but when I went into my home studio this morning, they were complete.

I don't remember finishing them, but that's nothing new. Dr. Young has told me about Drew, the one alter who's as artistic as me, so when stuff like this happens, I always assume it's his doing.

"When we talked last, you said you had another project lined up," I say, uncomfortable with her praise.

She returns the drawings to the large manilla envelope and sets it aside. "I think you're really gonna like this one. The book is about a little girl who meets a biker and gets scared because of the way he looks. By the end of the story, she realizes that he's a very nice man, and the lesson is to not judge a book by its cover."

Say what?

The description of this new project hits a little too close to home. I must be a glutton for punishment because rather than turn down the work like I should, I'm excited by the idea of something that allows me to think about Journey.

"I look forward to reading it," I say when she hands me the folder containing the story. "Does the author have any specific requests?"

"Nope. She's seen a lot of your previous work and trusts you to make the story come to life in a way that's appealing for kids."

We spend the next ten minutes discussing ideas, and by the time I leave, my nerves are buzzing with anticipation. I'm eager to get home and begin, but I have a few errands to run first. The grocery store is my main priority because I'm tired of leftovers and takeout.

As I meander through the aisles and randomly toss items into the cart, my brain is going a million miles a minute about this newest book. I already know exactly how I'm going to draw the biker thanks to my memories of Journey. But the little girl is another matter entirely.

An image of myself keeps filtering into my thoughts, but I refuse to do that. It seems too... personal.

I stop at the deli to get some lunch meat, and as I'm waiting for the girl to slice up my order, I scan my surroundings. My gaze lands on a familiar face, and my heart races, and the voices make themselves known.

What's he doing here?

Bikers have to eat, too.

Go talk to him!

He's not worth your time.

Journey is walking in my direction, and before he spots me, I turn around and race to the next aisle, my deli order forgotten.

What are you doing? He could be research.

Instead of running, you should drag him out to your car and ride him like he rides his Harley.

He's no damn good for you.

"Shut up," I snap.

"Excuse me?"

I whip my head to the left and force a smile at the elderly gentlemen staring at me.

"Oh, nothing," I say, a self-deprecating laugh escaping. "I was, uh, singing a song."

Singing a song? You're an idiot.

"Oh, I see," he says. "Well, have at it then."

He continues down the aisle in the opposite direction. Before I can make a bigger fool of myself, or worse, end up in Journey's sights, I head toward the registers. I've got enough in my cart to last a few days and can come back then.

"Wren?"

Journey's voice washes over me, sending warmth through my veins. Hating myself for reacting, I ignore him and move forward. Maybe he'll think I didn't hear him.

Yeah, right. Keep telling yourself that.

"You can run, but you can't hide," he says when he passes me as I enter a checkout lane.

"Did you find everything okay?" the cashier asks, giving me a reason to continue ignoring Journey.

"I, um…" I swallow, flustered. "Yes, I did."

I risk a glance over my shoulder. And Journey is nowhere to be seen. The voices quiet down slowly, until it's only my own thoughts I hear. After paying for my groceries, I quickly load them into my car and head home.

With my hands full, my steps falter when I reach my front door. There's a box on the ground, but I don't remember ordering anything. As soon as I deposit my bags inside, I return to the doorway and stare at the box like it's going to explode at any second.

C'mon, Wren. You have nothing to be afraid of.

I scoop up the package which is no bigger than a shoebox and carry it inside. It takes me a few more minutes to work up the courage to open it, and when I do, my breath catches in my throat.

Inside are two black carnations and a note. I carefully lift the paper and unfold it to read the words.

You can run, but you can't hide.

CHAPTER 15
JOURNEY

WHAT CAN YOU TELL ME ABOUT WREN ABBOTT?

"Fucker just picked his nose!"

I stifle my laugh at the indignation in Ghost's tone. We've been parked down the street from the Wingless Angels' road captain, Jester, for two hours, and I'm bored out of my mind. He's gone as far as his rickety front porch, and the most excitement there's been is his offensive nose-picking.

"At least he's not eating the boogers," I say dryly.

Ghost shakes his head. "How the hell is this club a threat? If the rest of them are anything like this guy, then we're dealing with overgrown toddlers."

"Crow says they're a threat, so we treat them like a damn threat."

"Yeah, yeah."

Ghost keeps his focus on Jester, and we let the silence take hold. It's been a while since we've had the need for a good old-fashioned stake out. I've always enjoyed them, but I've got other things I'd rather be doing.

Like Wren.

After seeing her at the grocery store and getting a very obvious brush-off, I returned to the clubhouse and dove into her therapist's notes. I want to understand her, but she's making it virtually impossible with her insistence that I stay away.

"Thank fuck," Ghost mutters, pulling me from my thoughts. "The cavalry has arrived."

I look in the rearview mirror and see the club's minivan parked behind us. Don't judge... A minivan allows us to surveil places where we'd otherwise stick out like a sore thumb.

Now that Screamer and Python are here, our shift is over. We fill them in on what we've observed, which admittedly is jack squat, before I turn on the Jeep's ignition and start to drive back to the clubhouse.

"What're you up to the rest of the day?" Ghost asks after a few minutes.

"I've gotta run an errand in Austin," I reply cryptically.

"Would this errand have anything to do with Wren?"

"And if it does?"

He lifts his hands in mock surrender. "No judgment here, bro. Just a question."

Heaving a sigh, I nod. "Yeah, it's got something to do with her."

"You're really gaga over her, aren't you?"

"Gaga?"

"You know what I mean." He chuckles. "Crow hit the nail on the head when he said things were gonna get interesting."

"I take it you'd handle things differently," I comment.

Surprisingly, I really *am* interested in his response. I value the opinions of my brothers above pretty much anyone else in the world, and maybe I need a little reassurance that I'm not as crazy as people think Wren is.

Ghost shrugs. "Don't know. I mean, my mom has Alzheimer's, and I guess that could be similar to Wren's disorder, but then again, there's really no comparison."

"Thanks. You're a big help," I mutter.

"Look, my mom is my mom, ya know? I'd do anything for her. Hell, I did by coming back to this town to take care of her. But a mom is different from an old lady. I'd like to think I'm the kinda guy who wouldn't give two shits about what issues the love of my life is dealing with, but I haven't been put in that position yet."

"Love of my life?" I repeat. "How'd we get to that?"

"Face it, Journey. You claimed her. You love her. Lord fucking knows why because you really do barely know her, but the heart wants what the heart wants. Sometimes, you just have to run with it and pray to all that's holy that you don't get sliced to pieces in the process."

"Damn, G." I whistle. "When did you get so wise?"

Pain crosses his features, but he quickly masks it. There's a story there, I'm sure of it, but I won't press. When he transferred from the Oregon chapter, Crow made it clear that Ghost would talk when he was ready, and we weren't to push. Pres said he's loyal to a fault and lives for the club, and that's all I need to know.

"So, what are ya gonna do in Austin?" he asks, returning to the original subject.

Having reached the clubhouse, I put the vehicle in park but make no move to get out.

"Wren's therapist is based there," I say.

"No," he breathes.

"What?"

"You can't go to her therapist."

"Why?"

"Confidentiality, for one." Ghost narrows his eyes at me. "And for two, that's crossing a major line."

"Bro, I've gotta do something. Wren's avoiding me like the plague. I've tried to call and text, and I've gone to her apartment a few times, and I'm getting nowhere. Maybe Dr. Young can help shed light on a way in."

"And if Wren finds out?"

"She won't," I say with more confidence than I feel. "Dr. Young won't even know I'm digging for information."

"How do ya figure?"

"I made an appointment under Sam Lincoln. The good doc thinks I'm a new patient."

"Of course, you'd use your legal name."

"It's not like I can use Journey. I'm not fucking Prince."

"Don't you get it? It doesn't matter what name you use. What you're doing is unethical."

"Because we live such an ethical life," I snort.

"I hope, for your sake, you know what you're doing," he says as he opens the passenger door. "Good luck."

It takes a little over an hour to get to Austin due

to traffic, and my conversation with Ghost plays on a loop in my head as I drive. Maybe he's right, and this is a fucked idea, but I'm running out of options.

After parking, I make my way inside the building and look at the directory to see which floor Dr. Young is on. Before I know it, I'm walking into her waiting room, which is empty. There's no receptionist, so I take a seat and wait.

Five minutes pass before a door opens, and two women step out.

"I'll see you next week," the older of the two says. She waits until the patient leaves, and then looks at me. "Sam?"

I rise to my feet and thrust my hand out to shake hers. "Yep, that's me."

"Give me a few minutes, and then we can get started." I sit back down to wait some more, and I replay the cover story I came up with until the door opens again. "Come on in."

I follow her into the room and am surprised to see it set up cozier than I expected.

"Have a seat," she instructs. Once I'm across from her, she lifts a pad of paper from the small table next to her chair and rests it on her lap. "So, what brings you here?"

I open my mouth to recite my cover story, but

none of those details are what comes out of my mouth. Instead, I blurt the one thing guaranteed to get me into hot water.

"What can you tell me about Wren Abbott?"

CHAPTER 16
WREN

Remember, Wren... a biker is a biker is a biker. They're all the same.

"How have you been since your last appointment?"

My leg bounces, vibrating the couch in Dr. Young's office. It's been two days since I saw Journey at the grocery store and got that package, and I've been full of nervous energy ever since. Coming here is the first time I've left my apartment since then, and I was looking in the rearview mirror the entire drive. It's a wonder I made it here alive.

"Wren, what is it?" she asks when I don't respond. "Did something happen?"

"What?"

"You seem distracted," she says. "Did something happen that is upsetting you?"

I shake my head as I rest my hand on my thigh, silently willing it to stop bouncing.

"Wren?"

"Yeah, yeah, it's me." I wring my hands in my lap and make a snap decision. "I saw Journey again." Dr. Young tenses at my statement, and I hone in on that. "What?"

She leans forward and levels me with a look that makes my anxiety deepen. "Before you go any further, there's something I need to tell you. But before I do, I want you to remember that you're in a safe space." I open my mouth but no words come out, so she continues. "Journey came to see me yesterday."

I shoot to my feet. "What? But… why? How?"

"Sit down, Wren," she orders. "Remember that this is a safe space."

My chest heaves, but I do as she says and sit. "Why would he come see you? How does he even know about you?"

"From what I could gather, he wanted to know more about you." She holds her hand up to keep me silent. "Now, I didn't tell him anything. I would never do that. But I thought you should know."

"I don't understand," I cry. "What does he want from me? When I said I saw him again, I didn't specify that it happened twice." I tell her about our encounters, about his vow to not give up, and about the fact that I'm pretty sure he witnessed a switch." I take a deep breath before launching into a recount of the package on my doorstep. "I'm just... I don't know."

"And you think the package was from him?"

"Who else would it be? The note said the same thing that he said to me in the store."

"Okay. Let's back up a bit and take things one at a time, okay?" she suggests, and I nod. "When you initially saw Journey again, how did it make you feel?"

I shrug. "I guess I was excited, which scared me."

"Why did it scare you?"

"Why wouldn't it?" I counter. "I'm broken, Doc. All I have to give is good sex."

"That's not true," she insists. "Wren, your diagnosis is not who you are."

I laugh humorlessly. "Uh, I'm pretty sure my diagnosis is exactly that."

"You know what I mean. Plenty of people with Dissociative Identity Disorder live normal lives and have normal relationships. Your disorder doesn't have to define your life."

"I don't think a relationship with the man who's stalking me is exactly smart."

"Probably not," she agrees. "But he's not the only man out there."

He's the only one who's stuck around long enough for me to be confused as hell.

"It doesn't matter," I say. "Even if I do like him, he's a biker. I'd never fit in with his lifestyle. And that's assuming he isn't a threat to me like his stalking suggests."

"You keep saying he's stalking you," she points out. "Have you made a police report?"

"No."

"Why not?"

Why not, indeed?

"I… Well…" I lower my head and fiddle with my hands. "Because he'd never actually hurt me."

Dr. Young clears her throat, but I refuse to look at her.

"Kirby?" she asks. "No, wait… Annie?"

"Kirby hasn't been around lately," I say. "He's afraid of the biker guy. But I'm not."

"So it is you, Annie." I nod, and Dr. Young continues. "You've met Journey?" Again, I nod. "And you're not afraid of him?"

"No. He promised he would always protect me."

"He did?"

Finally, I lift my head. "Yeah. He said he's not a

liar, so he can make promises. He also didn't let Daddy hurt me or Wren, so he's nice."

"Did you know that I met him, too?"

My eyes widen. "You did?"

"I did," she says. "He came to talk to me about Wren."

"I think he likes her. She's a little afraid of him, and I keep trying to tell her he's okay, but she doesn't hear me."

"Maybe I could tell her for you," she suggests. "Could you get her for me, and I'll do that?"

"I'll try." I squeeze my eyes shut and concentrate real hard. When I raise my chin, I stare at Dr. Young, who's watching me intently. "What?" I ask.

"We were talking about a police report."

"Right." I shake my head. "No, I haven't filed one. His actions tell me I should, but something is holding me back."

"I think a part of you trusts him."

I squint at her as if that will make her words make sense. "You just told me he came here yesterday asking about me, and he left me that package. Now you sound like you think I should invite him to live with me. Make up your mind, doc."

My snippy tone isn't lost on me, but I have enough going on in my head without the one sane person who's supposed to help me, making things more confusing.

"It's not my mind that needs to be made up. Look, I can't tell you what to do. That's not what therapy is about. But I'm also not going to let you flounder."

"Okay."

"What if you file a police report and let them do their job?" she suggests. "If he's not a threat, they'll determine that for you. If he is, then you'll be protected."

I consider it and decide it's a logical solution. "I'll go to the station tomorrow."

"Good." Dr. Young leans back and relaxes in her chair. "Now, we've got a few more minutes before our time is up. Is there anything specific you want to talk about?"

We spend the rest of the session going through the steps of what I can expect when I make the report, and by the time I leave, I'm feeling less anxious. Unfortunately, it doesn't last because as soon as I walk into my apartment, my cell phone rings.

"Hello?"

"This is a call from…"

I listen to the prison's recording, fully intending

to hang up, but my gut shouts at me to stay on the line.

"'Bout time you accepted my call," my father gripes once the recording ends.

"What do you want?" I ask, resigned to at least a short conversation.

As much as I despise the man, he *is* my father.

You owe him nothing.

"I had your Uncle Craig leave something for you," he says, and my mind flashes to the carnations and note. "He said you'll find it in the nightstand in your bedroom."

A shiver runs through me at the thought of Uncle Craig in my home, and I make my way to my room. Pulling open the nightstand drawer, I gasp and stumble backward.

"What the fuck do I need a gun for?" I demand.

Dad chuckles, and it scares me just as it did when I was a child. "If you're gonna be hanging around with bikers, you better be able to protect yourself."

With those parting words, he disconnects the call. Question after question runs through my mind, not the least of which is how my dad or Uncle Craig found me. I've done everything I can to make sure my address isn't listed anywhere they could find it.

After slamming the drawer shut, I stomp out to

the living room and curl up on the couch to ponder the situation I find myself in. It isn't long before I'm having an internal debate with myself about reaching out to Journey, but I quickly dismiss the idea.

Remember, Wren… a biker is a biker is a biker. They're all the same.

CHAPTER 17
JOURNEY

I'll do whatever it takes to protect you.

"You about done?"

I glance up at Screamer, who's wiping the grease from his hands with a rag. We both work for a local mechanic, and our specialty is motorcycles. I'm finishing up a Harley Softail, but apparently, I'm not going fast enough for him.

"Should be in a few minutes," I tell him. "Just want to double-check everything before signing off on completion."

"Well, there's a woman out front, and she's asking for you."

I lift my head so fast I'm surprised I don't get whiplash. "A woman?"

Screamer smirks. "Judging by the level of rage

and disgust in her expression, I'm guessing she's some chick you fucked and ducked."

Chuckling, I shake my head. "This can't be good."

"Definitely not. Be glad Jared isn't here today," he says, referring to our boss. "I've got a feeling there's about to be a big scene."

After setting my tools down, I rise to my feet and stretch, buying myself a few seconds before I come face to face with someone who apparently hates me.

When I step into the front of the shop, my stomach drops.

"Wren?"

"Wait," Screamer says as he steps up next to me. "This is Wren?"

Wren stares at me with fury as I respond, and I notice she's holding a brown paper bag close to her chest. "Uh, yeah, this is Wren."

Screamer throws his head back and laughs. "I was right. There's definitely gonna be a fucking scene."

"Walk away, Screamer," I order.

"Aw, c'mon, Jou—"

"Walk. Away," I bark.

"Buzzkill," he mutters as he returns to the shop area.

"I gotta say, I'm surprised to see you," I comment when Wren and I are alone.

"Really?" she lashes out. "You leave this in my home, and you thought I'd let it slide."

Wren sets the bag on the counter and gently slides it toward me. Her movements are so slow and in complete contraction with the malice in her tone. I look in the bag, and my own rage surfaces.

"Where'd you get that?" I demand.

"Like you don't know," she snaps. "It was in my nightstand, right where you left it."

"I have no idea what you're talking about." I reach behind my back and pull my own gun from my waistband to show her. "I've got my piece. There's no way I'd have left it behind."

"You didn't leave anything behind. You broke into my apartment and put it right where he told you to."

"Where who told me to?"

"Don't play dumb, Journey."

I take a few steps back, lean against the wall, and cross my arms over my chest. "I'm not playing dumb, Wren. I don't know what the hell you're talking about."

She rolls her eyes. "And I suppose you're gonna tell me that you didn't leave me the flowers and note."

"What flowers and note?"

Wren throws her arms up and begins to pace. I

keep a close eye on her every step, watching for any indication that anyone other than Wren is present. I don't know what specific triggers she has for a switch, and I'm not at all sure I want to find out when she's this pissed.

"And then there's the matter of your little visit to Dr. Young," she shouts, no longer trying to keep her voice down. "What is wrong with you?"

Well, shit. I knew that was gonna come back to bite me in the ass.

"Listen, I won't deny that," I say. "And I'm sorry. But you didn't leave me much choice."

"Did it ever occur to you that I want nothing to do with you?"

No. It didn't.

Instead of voicing my thought, I push off the wall and walk around the counter. I block her from pacing, but when she flinches, I take a step back.

"What are you doing?" she demands.

"Do you want nothing to do with me?" I ask.

That gets her attention, and she halts. "What?"

"Do you want nothing to do with me?" I repeat. "It's a simple question, Wren."

"I…" She shakes her head. "I don't know."

"If you really want me to back off, I will," I tell her honestly while simultaneously hoping like hell she doesn't.

"You will?"

"Of course. I'd never force you to do anything you don't want to do."

"But the flowers? And the note?"

"Yeah, about those… I really don't know what you're talking about."

"And the gun?"

"Nope."

"But my dad…"

I stiffen. "What's he got to do with this?"

"He called me and said Uncle Craig left it. I haven't seen Uncle Craig in years, and there's no way either of them know where I live, so I assumed he meant you." She locks eyes with me. "You're working for him, aren't you?"

"Wren, I've never met your dad. All I know about him is what I've read about his crimes."

She sighs, her shoulders slumping. "But I… I'm so confused."

"Why don't you start at the beginning?" I suggest. "Tell me about the flowers and note."

And she does. It takes everything in me not to punch holes in the walls as she speaks. I hate that there's someone out there who made her question my intentions, someone who is a real danger to her.

"And then last night, my dad called and told me about the gun," she says, finishing her explanation.

Nothing makes sense, but I'm not sure that she could explain it any better than she has. She clearly had assumptions that were very wrong about it all.

"I promise you, I had nothing to do with any of it," I tell her. "I'd never do anything to hurt you, Wren. Quite the opposite. I'll do whatever it takes to protect you."

Before I know what's happening, Wren has me shoved against the front window of the shop, her fingers wrapped as far around my throat as they'll go.

"Wren doesn't need your fucking protection."

CHAPTER 18
WREN

I don't need you or the Soulless Kings.

"You're not Wren."

I smirk at the man in my grasp. "No shit, Sherlock. She's weak, and would never know how to stand up to you."

"Can you at least tell me who I'm dealing with?"

Rage boils my blood at his ability to speak when I'm trying like hell to squeeze the life out of him. Damn, Wren and her little body.

"Not that it matters, but I'm Aaron."

He narrows his eyes at me as if trying to decipher my words, and then he grins. "Oh, right. I read about you."

"The fuck?"

"You fancy yourself Wren's big bad bodyguard," he taunts.

"I've protected her since she was five years old, you stupid prick," I bite out. "And I'll protect her until the day she dies."

"Hate to break it to you," he sneers. "But Wren doesn't need you. She's got me."

"And you're the same as the man who broke her."

I draw my arm back and attempt a right hook, but Journey stops my hand with his.

"You're damn lucky that whatever happens to you happens to her. Otherwise, I'd end you."

"As if you could."

Journey stares at me for a long moment, and then he surprises me when his face softens. "You don't need to keep Wren safe from me. I'd never hurt her."

"That's what Stone said, and she barely managed to survive him."

His expression hardens in an instant. "Did you say Stone?"

"Who else would I have said?" I snap. "Her father broke her, and now she's risking what's left of herself on you… another biker."

"You need to let Wren come back," he says, panicking. "Get her, now!"

"That's not how it works."

"Aaron, please. You've gotta see that she's safe

with me. I haven't hurt her yet, have I? And I've had opportunity."

I consider his words and still, I hesitate. "How the fuck am I supposed to know I can trust you?"

Journey moves away from me and runs a hand through his hair. "Have you ever heard the expression '*the enemy of my enemy is my friend*'?"

"Of course. Who hasn't?"

"Well, Stone is my enemy, my club's enemy. So, wouldn't that make me Wren's friend?"

His logic might be twisted, but it's hard to argue with. Unfortunately, before I can reply, I'm yanked from the forefront.

My muscles ache from all the tension running through my body, and I make a conscious effort to relax as I glance at my surroundings.

"Wren?" Journey is in front of me in an instant, his hands cupping my cheeks. "Are you back?"

"It happened, didn't it?" I ask, embarrassment settling in.

"Yeah, but it's okay."

I pull away from him and sit in one of the chairs lined up against a wall where customers can wait while their vehicle is worked on. I've spent so much energy trying to avoid Journey, and here I am, switching in front of him again.

"It's not okay." I hand my head. "Who, um…"

"Aaron."

"Shit." I lift my eyes to his. "I'm sorry if I… if he… What happened?"

"Nothing bad, sweetheart," he reassures as he squats in front of me. "He was just trying to protect you. But I think we came to an understanding."

Uncertainty niggles at my brain. "What kind of understanding?"

"That he doesn't have to protect you anymore because I'm here to do it for him."

I shove him away from me. "I don't need you to pro—"

"Tell me about your dad."

"What?"

"Your dad… tell me about him."

"What can I say that you don't already know?" I counter. "You say you don't work with him, but I don't know if I believe you."

"Wren, I don't work with or for him, I swear. Just the opposite, in fact."

"What's that supposed to mean?"

Rather than answer my questions, he asks one of his own. "What's your dad's name?"

I scoff. "Ryan Abbott. Why?"

"Right, but what's his road name?"

"He doesn't have one."

"Does the name Stone sound familiar to you?"

I close my eyes and try to think back to when I was a child. There isn't much I remember about my family beyond what I've read or been told. But one thing that surfaces, blinking at me like a neon sign on the fritz, is an image of my dad wearing… a cut.

My hands fly to my mouth. "He was a biker."

"And if I'm right, he's the president of the Wingless Angels MC."

Frantically, I shake my head. "But he can't be. He's been in prison for twenty years. How would he run an MC from a cell?"

"I've heard of crazier things."

"No. That's nuts. I mean…" I tilt my head and stare at Journey. "Oh my God. Is that why you scare me? Because my mind recognized the similarity between you and him?"

"I'd say that's probably a pretty safe bet." He smiles, and I shiver. "Do I really scare you?"

"Yeah. A little," I admit. "But you also intrigue me. Which, I gotta say, is a bit disconcerting."

"Disconcerting?" He snorts. "Such a big word."

"If all of this is true, what could my dad possibly want from me now? I haven't seen him since the day of the…" I swallow past the lump in my throat. "Let's just say it's been a while."

"I think he's kept tabs on you for all these years, and now he's found a way you can be useful to him." Regret flashes in his eyes, but he forges ahead. "Sorry, that sounds cold. But I doubt he has a selfless bone in his body."

"It sounds cold because it is. But it's also the truth."

"I know you probably won't understand, but I have to take this information to the Soulless Kings. They need to know."

"I don't think so," I snap, moving toward the door. "This is my life, Journey. And I don't want the details used as a punchline for your club."

"Wren, no. That's not what it is. But the Wingless Angels are gunning for us, and the only way to stop them is to take out their leader."

"In other words, you wanna kill my dad," I summarize.

"Well… yeah."

"Look, I don't give a rat's ass about his life or what happens to him," I begin. "But I do care about mine. Just leave it alone."

"I can't do that. I swear, nothing will happen to you because of this. I won't let it."

Needing to get away from him, away from the reality of all that's come to light, I push the door open.

"I don't need you or the Soulless Kings," I say over my shoulder. "I'm a big girl and can take care of myself, despite what you may think."

CHAPTER 19
JOURNEY

As long as I'm a Soulless King, anyone associated with me is fair game in the eyes of our enemies.

"Still playing the long game?"

I down the rest of my Dr. Pepper and glare at Connor, the prospect working the bar at the clubhouse tonight. It's been a few weeks since Wren confronted me at the shop, and I've spent every free minute trying to win her over. I've called, texted, sent flowers, and even went so far as to go to her apartment and talk to her through her door when she wouldn't open it. And my efforts are being rewarded because she finally agreed to get together tonight.

"Always," I say with a grunt as I tap out another text.

> Me: Can't wait to see you

I wait a few minutes for her customary 'leave me alone' reply, and when it doesn't come, I take it as a win.

"Gotta say, Journey," Conner states, pulling my attention away from my phone. "I definitely didn't see you as the type to settle down, but it looks good on you."

"Are you hitting on me, prospect?" I taunt.

His eyes widen, and his shoulders tense. "What? No! I'm a pussy guy for sure."

I bust out laughing. "If you're gonna become a Soulless King, ya gotta learn how to take a fucking joke."

Conner throws a towel at me before moving away to get drinks for a few of the club whores. The way he's flirting with them tells me my joke really hit a nerve. Dude's going so hard, it's like he has a point to prove.

"What time are you heading out?" Jackyl asks when he steps up beside me and slaps me on the back.

I glance at the time on my cell. "Few minutes. What's up?"

"My dick as soon as I get to Leah's," he replies.

"Jesus, that's more info than I need."

"Figure you gotta get your kicks somehow. Ever since you hooked up with Wren, you haven't so much as flirted with a club whore. And judging by your ever-present grumpy mood, I'm guessing you haven't gotten laid either."

I push to my feet. "And on that note, I'm outta here."

Jackyl's laughter follows me as I head out the door to my Harley. His observations piss me off because they're the truth. From the moment I saw Wren, no other woman compared. When my attention isn't on club business and the Wingless Angels threat, it's on her.

The ride to Wren's apartment seems to take forever, but I'm pretty sure my impatience is the cause. Traffic wasn't bad, and I maintained a healthy pace well above the speed limit.

When I knock on her door, the nerves start to settle in, making me feel like a teenage boy picking up his prom date.

Get a grip. You're a one percenter. If you can handle that, you can handle this.

"You're early," Wren says as she yanks the door open.

"Hello to you, too," I tease.

She pushes at one side of her hair and rocks back on her heels.

Ah, she's flustered.

"C'mon in."

I close and lock the door behind me, and when I turn back around to face her, she's staring at me like I'm an alien from another planet.

"What?"

Wren shakes her head as she puts a hand to her throat. "Oh, um… nothing."

"You should take a picture," I advise. "It'd last longer."

That taunt does the trick. Her body relaxes, and she narrows her eyes at me. "You're impossible," she sasses. "Gimme a minute to finish getting ready, then we can go."

"Actually, I was thinking we'd stay here."

"You've been hounding me to go out with you, and now you don't want to go out?"

The way her nose wrinkles with annoyance is fucking cute as hell, and it takes everything in me not to close the distance between us and kiss her senseless. Instead, I remind myself why I don't want to actually take her out, and my lust cools.

"It's not that I don't want to take you out," I explain. "But things are heating up with the Wingless Angels, and now that all the puzzle pieces have clicked as far as Stone being your dad, I think it's best we don't tempt the devil."

"What do you mean, things are heating up?" Fear enters her eyes. "I haven't gotten any more packages or calls."

"And I hope you never do. But all the cards are on the table now, and war has been declared. Stone and his brothers are out for blood, and I'm fairly certain it doesn't matter who gets caught up in the bloodshed."

"You think they'd try something while we're on a date?"

"I think they'd try something if we were in a packed church on Easter Sunday," I counter.

"Oh."

"Look, I'm not going to take any risks where you're concerned. I can protect you, but I'm still just one person. I'd prefer to have my brothers at our backs out in public."

"I hate to point this out, but if we can't leave my apartment, how would anything long-term even work between us?"

"The Wingless Angels aren't gonna be around forever, Wren," I tell her. "And once they're out of the picture, the threat is gone."

"I've seen the tv shows, Journey," she counters hotly. "I know what that one percent patch on your cut means. There will always be a threat, and I can't live like that. Not with what I already have to deal with on a daily basis."

It irks me to no end that she's right. As long as I'm a Soulless King, anyone associated with me is fair game in the eyes of our enemies.

"I'll leave the club then," I blurt.

Shock rocks me to the core that I'd even consider it, but as the idea blossoms in my head, it takes root.

"Why?" she cries. "I'm nobody special. Hell, I'm fourteen nobodies."

I chuckle. "I'd leave if it meant a chance at a life with you."

"But we don't know each other!"

"And I'm trying to change that," I snap.

"No. No, I can't ask you to do that. I may not have grown up in the biker world, but I know that for someone like you, it's everything."

We stare at each other for a moment, both of us silently pleading with the other to back down. When she doesn't, I make a decision that could have horrible consequences.

"On second thought, we are going out," I tell her. "Go finish getting ready."

"Where are we going?"

"You'll see."

CHAPTER 20
WREN

No one's ever stuck around.

"What're you waiting for?"

My gaze is fixed on Journey's Harley, and as tempted as I am to hop on, I'm also a little frightened. I've never been on a motorcycle before.

"You just got done telling me why you didn't want to be out in public because of the danger, and now you expect me to just ride off into the sunset with you?" I shake my head. "I don't think so."

"We're not gonna be in public," he assures me. "And I promise I'll stick to the speed limit."

His devilish grin does nothing to alleviate my concerns, but it does send a shiver of need up my spine.

"If I die, I'm gonna haunt your ass," I grumble as I let him help me onto the bike.

"You'll be the sexiest ghost I've ever seen."

"Not helping."

He laughs and throws his leg over the seat to settle in front of me. "Wrap your arms around my waist and hold on tight."

And I do, although I'm not sure digging my nails into his abdomen is what he had in mind as far as holding on tight.

"Here we are," he says when he parks next to a large building fifteen minutes later. "Home sweet home."

"You live here?"

"It's the clubhouse, so yeah."

Unease twists my stomach into knots. "Why would you bring me here?" I swivel my head and take in all the other motorcycles and vehicles parked in the gravel lot and yard. "This is too much, Journey. I can't do this. What if I…"

"What if you what?" he asks gently.

I sigh dramatically. "What if I switch?"

"Do you trust me?"

"No. I don't fucking know you!"

"Aw, c'mon, Wren," he cajoles. "Have I let you down yet?"

"Well… no. But that doesn't mean you won't."

He reaches for my hand and flattens it over his chest. "I will not let anyone do or say anything to hurt you, okay? You have my word."

And there's the rub. Words are just words. Actions are a true measure of the man.

And you'll never know if Journey is a man of his word if you don't give him a chance to show you with his actions.

"Stupid voices," I mutter.

"Wait, you can hear them?" he asks, his eyes wide.

Taking a step back, I wave my hand dismissively. "Yeah, sometimes."

"What's it like?"

The curiosity in his tone strikes a chord, and my heart melts a little. "I don't know. It's normal to me, I guess. If I had to compare it to something, I'd say it's like I have a dozen different podcasts playing in my head, trying to compete for my attention. Rarely is it all of them at once, but you get the idea."

"That's gotta be hard."

I snort. "Ya think?"

"Sorry."

"Don't you get it? I struggle enough, but if I'm thrust into the middle of a crowd, all hell could break loose."

"You go to Ballinger's," he points out. "They get crowded."

"But Ballinger's is familiar. It took me a while to be able to go without freaking out or switching. And even though it's a safe place for me, the alters still take over sometimes."

"The clubhouse can become a safe place, too."

It would be nice to expand my zone of comfort. What Journey's offering could give me a life I thought I was incapable of having, one I never thought I deserved.

But at what cost?

Deciding to throw caution to the wind, at least for tonight, I nod. "Fine. I'll go in. But you better not leave my side."

Journey throws an arm around my shoulder, and warmth spreads throughout my body.

"Wouldn't dream of it."

Journey leads me inside, and I'm immediately hit with what feels like a solid wall of music and smoke. I must tense under his arm because he leads me to the opposite wall where there's a jukebox, and he yanks the cord from the wall.

Silence fills the room as all eyes turn to us. I squirm under the scrutiny, but Journey just tightens his hold, offering whatever comfort he can.

"What the fuck, J?" a man shouts angrily.

"Listen up," Journey says loudly. "I've got an announcement to make."

Aw, hell.

"What? Did that chick finally let you sink your cock into her again?" another man says as he walks toward us.

Journey moves so fast, and the next thing I know, the guy is flat on the floor with blood coming from his nose.

"Wren isn't just some chick," Journey snarls. "And the next time you choose to speak about her like that, you'll be out in the cold. Got it, Blain?"

"Yeah, yeah. Got it."

"Anyone else have an opinion they wanna share?" Journey asks. No one says a word. "Good. Now, my announcement. I've already told the officers, but the rest of you need to know that Wren is mine, and I expect you to treat her with the same respect as you do Addison." He glances at me and winks. "And if you can't do that, I'm gone."

"You're what?" a third man snarls as he moves from the bar to stand in front of Journey. "I don't think I heard you right."

"You heard me just fine, Crow."

"You'd really walk?"

"In a heartbeat."

Crow stares at him for a moment before turning his attention to me. "Wren?"

"Uh, y-yes," I stutter, doing my best not to let the voices win the struggle for control.

Crow smiles and strides toward me. "I'm Crow, the president of these yahoos. It's nice to meet you."

"It… What?"

He chuckles. "I take it you weren't expecting to be welcomed with open arms."

"Well, yeah. I mean… You do know that Stone is my dad, right?" I lean close and whisper, "And I'm kinda crazy."

He erupts into laughter, and I can't help but wonder what is so funny. I'm sweating bullets, and he's acting like this is all normal.

"You're gonna fit in just fine, Wren," he finally says when his laughter subsides. "Welcome to the family."

"I… thanks."

Crow spins around to face Journey, who's grinning like an idiot. "As for you, VP… You're not goin' anywhere. Soulless Kings stick together, no matter what."

"I know, Pres. But she didn't, and I needed to show her."

"Yeah, I get that. Helluva way to get a point across, though."

"Whatever it takes."

"You heard him," Crow shouts to the entire room. "Wren is one of us. Anyone who can't accept that, there's the door." He points to the exit.

Not a single person moves in that direction. Quite the contrary. One by one, I'm engulfed in hugs by big, burly men who all seem to genuinely be happy about me being here.

Huh.

When I'm released by a man who introduced himself as Fudge, Journey takes his place.

"Told ya," he whispers in my ear. "So, whaddya say, Wren? Wanna give this a shot?"

I take a step back to lock eyes with him. "Under one condition."

"What's that?"

"If you ever decide you want out, you have to be honest with me," I tell him. "I don't want you to stick around out of some misguided sense of pity."

"Pity? Is that really what you think makes people stick around?"

"Honestly, I don't know because no one's ever stuck around."

CHAPTER 21
JOURNEY

That's the point.

No one's ever stuck around.

As we hang out at the clubhouse, those words play on a loop in my thoughts. Wren hasn't had an easy life, but the full impact didn't really sink in until she said that. It makes sense, I suppose. I'm sure there are plenty of people out there who would be running for the hills when they learn of her disorder.

But not me. If anything, it makes me want to be around her even more. Some might say I've got a hero complex, or I just want to fix her, but that couldn't be further from the truth. Wren is incredible. The fact that she's still standing after what she survived is a testament to the kind of person she is.

She is exactly the kind of woman I want by my side. And bonus, life will *never* be dull.

"I can see why you like her."

I shift my gaze from the corner where Wren is talking to Addison and grin at Ghost. "Liking her is the easy part," I confess. "Getting her to like me back is what took so damn long."

"Yeah, well, love ain't easy."

"And you know this how?" I ask, again sensing that there's a story there.

Rather than answer, he lifts his glass in salute. "I'm happy for ya, bro."

He makes his way out of the common area, and I consider following him, but dismiss the idea quickly because I promised Wren I wouldn't leave her.

I watch her for a few minutes, and when she shakes her head at Addison and Pres's old lady walks away, I make my way toward her.

"Everything okay?" I ask Wren.

"Yep."

I nod at her glass. "You've barely touched your drink."

"I'm sorry. I hate to waste it, but I don't like to drink too much alcohol with my meds. Especially if I'm in stressful situations."

"And you're in a stressful situation?"

Wren wrinkles her nose as she seems to contemplate that for a second. "Actually, no. Things are good."

"Told ya."

"Shut up."

"Listen, it's getting late. I can take you home if you want," I say casually. "Or you could stay here."

"Like a sleepover?" she teases, and the flirt from the first night we met comes out.

Leaning in, I lick a path up her neck to her earlobe. "Won't be doing much sleeping if I've got anything to say about it."

Wren turns her head and lightly brushes her lips over mine. "And what exactly would we be doing?"

I lift her over my shoulder, and she squeals. "I think I can show you better than I can tell you."

I carry her to my room and kick the door shut behind me. As soon as I set her on her feet, she's on me like bark on a tree. Her hands are everywhere, and she pushes me against the wall.

She didn't take the lead the last time, and hesitation has me gripping her arms and moving her back a little.

"Wren?" I ask, needing to know it's really her.

"Yeah," she says. "It's me."

That's all I need to hear. I rip her clothes from her body and toss them to the floor. She doesn't protest, and when she's standing before me naked,

I take a few minutes to appreciate all she has to offer.

"You are so beautiful." Wren reaches for my belt, but I block her and ease her back toward the bed. "Not yet, sweetheart. Let me enjoy you first."

She groans with frustration. I push her onto the mattress and drop to my knees. A moan escapes past her lips when my tongue swirls around her clit, and she grabs my head to hold me close.

I've always prided myself on taking care of my partner first, but I don't know how long I can hold out with Wren. I've been fantasizing about being with her again for weeks, and now that it's happening, my cock is straining against my zipper, begging to be inside her.

"Gonna make this fast, sweetheart," I say against her core.

I shove a finger inside her, working her from the inside and outside. Flicking my tongue over her clit as fast as I can, I pay attention to her reaction. It doesn't take long for her legs to quiver around my head, and her moans of ecstasy to fill the room.

Wren spasms around my finger, and when she starts to relax, I remove it and stand up. I lick the taste of her off my lips as I rush to strip, watching her the entire time.

She stretches her arms over her head, and I trail

my gaze from her satisfied expression to her tits. I linger over every inch of her, letting it sink in how lucky I am that it's me who she chose to give a chance to.

"Take a picture. It'll last longer," she says, throwing my own words back at me.

"Oh, I will. I'll take lots of 'em," I assure her. "But not now. Now, I'm gonna fuck you until there's no room in your head for anyone or anything but you and me."

"Sounds like heaven," she murmurs.

I climb on top of her, pinning her arms in place with one hand and lining myself up with her entrance with the other. Wren's tight pussy envelopes me in slick heat, and it's my turn to moan.

Fear of coming too soon has me freezing above her, but she doesn't let that stand. Wren moves her hips, forcing me to engage, and by some miracle, I don't explode.

"Thought you said this was gonna be fast," she purrs before nipping at my neck.

"You asked for it."

I increase my speed, thrusting in and out of her in a rhythm as old as time. The world around us fades away, and the only thing that matters is the perfection between us.

Reaching between our bodies, I press my thumb

to her clit and rub circles around it as we fuck. My ears ring, and her moans of desire seem to come from somewhere in the distance. Haze fills my vision, and a tingle skitters down my spine.

Knowing that I'm close, I push into her faster and harder. Her walls clamp around me, and she arches off the mattress as a wave of pleasure crashes over me. We ride the wave together, a tandem trip to a place of euphoria.

"Just as I remembered," she says when I collapse to her side.

"So you have thought about it," I tease.

She smacks me playfully on the chest. "Of course, I have. I'm damaged, not dead."

I lift onto my elbow and glare at her. "Don't talk about yourself like that. You're not damaged. Fuck, you're so not damaged." Cupping her cheek, I press a kiss to her lips. "You're unique and strong and sexy and brave and smart and talented… Should I go on?"

Wren grins. "I mean, you shouldn't stop."

I throw my leg over hers and pull her close. "I'll never stop showing you how special you are."

"A girl could get used to this," she says as she snuggles against me.

"That's the point."

CHAPTER 22
WREN

Somehow, I know you'd never hurt me.

"Morning."

Journey's deep voice filters through my lingering drowsiness, and I smile at him. We didn't get much sleep, my body is reminding me of what we *did* do, and I'm… happy.

"Hey."

He settles his mouth over mine, and for a split-second, I think about pushing him away until I've had a chance to brush my teeth, but the thought quickly disappears. I get lost in his taste, his smell… him.

And in an instant, that all changes.

Kaboom!

The bed shakes, and my ears ring. Journey is on

his feet in a flash, and he grabs a gun from the nightstand.

How'd I miss that?

"Stay here," he commands as he pulls a pair of sweats on and makes his way out of the room.

It's on the tip of my tongue to argue, but I don't. I scramble up the mattress, pulling the blanket up to my chin as I go, and watch as brother after brother runs past the open door.

What is happening?

Chaos permeates the air, fills the clubhouse to the brim. Panic sets in, and my mind races.

Told ya he was trouble.

He'll keep you safe.

Fuck, he was hot-naked.

You're gonna die if you stay with him.

He's gonna die if he stays with you.

"Shut up!" I scream, covering my face with my hands.

"Wren?"

I peek between my fingers and see Addi coming toward me. Tears prick my eyes, and my chin wobbles. "What is happening?"

"Nothing we can't handle," she says, climbing onto the bed beside me.

"Maybe you can handle it, but…" I shake my head. "I'm not so sure about me."

"Girl, you're made of tough stuff. And you've got all of us to help. Trust me when I say, you can handle it."

I lower my hands and look at her. "What exactly is *it*?"

She tucks her hair behind her ear and sighs. "A bomb."

"A bomb?!"

Addi twists and rests her hands on my shoulders as if anchoring me to Earth. "It wasn't a big one, and no one was hurt."

"A bomb is a bomb. Who gives a damn if it's a big one or not?"

She chuckles. "True. And if my colleagues find out I was here when it went off, I'll be buried in paperwork. I told Crow we should've gone home last night."

"Wait. You don't live here?"

"No. We stay here sometimes, but we have a house."

"But I thought you had to live here."

"Nope," she says, popping the 'p'.

"Oh. Good to know." I roll my eyes. "Fuck, what is wrong with me? A bomb just exploded, and I'm sitting here talking about living arrangements."

"Nothing is wrong with you," Addi insists. "I'm

guessing it's your brain's way of working through the muck."

"Working through the muck," I repeat. "I like that."

"Why don't we go out and see if we can help with anything?" she suggests.

"Yeah, that'd be good. Let me just throw some clothes on, and I'll be right out."

Bobbing her brows, she smirks. "You're naked under there, aren't you?"

"Yep."

"I bet Journey is pissed as hell that he got pulled out of bed with you here."

With that, she gets to her feet and leaves the room, pulling the door shut behind her. I throw the blanket off of me and swing my legs over the bed. The last thing I wanna do is put dirty clothes on, so I trudge to Journey's dresser to find something suitable to wear.

Settling on a pair of sweats with a drawstring and an overly large t-shirt, I get dressed. I wish I had time to at least shower, but who am I kidding? No one's gonna care what I look like when they're dealing with the aftermath of an explosion.

Just as I'm about to walk out of the room, a ping reaches my ears. Thinking it's my cell, I retrace my steps and pick the phone up off the nightstand.

When I tap the screen to bring it to life, my blood runs cold.

> Unknown: Stay away from my daughter or the next time, the bomb will be inside

My legs buckle, and I crumble to the floor. I manage to use the bed for support, and stare at what I now know is Journey's cell, not mine.

How did he know? How'd he get this number?

"What's wrong?"

I lift my head and see Journey kneeling in front of me. He must be an expert at stealth because I didn't even hear him come in.

"My, uh…" I swallow and try to gather my thoughts. Turning the phone so he can see the text, I say, "Stone texted you."

His entire body tenses as he reads. "Sonofabitch!"

I flinch at his rage, and he immediately forces himself to relax and engulfs me in his arms.

"I'm sorry," he says. "I didn't mean to scare you."

"It's okay. Really. Somehow, I know you'd never hurt me. It was just an involuntary reaction."

"I wish I could stay here with you, but there's a lot to do," he says, pulling back so he can look me in the eye. "Do you want me to get someone to take you home?"

"No. I can help with whatever needs done."

"Are you sure?"

"Yeah."

"Okay. Crow's called an emergency meeting. But I'll get back to you as soon as I can, okay?" I nod. "By the way, you look sexy as fuck in my clothes."

Heat rushes into my cheeks.

"Thanks."

CHAPTER 23
JOURNEY

One day at a fucking time.

"How'd they get close enough to the clubhouse to plant that bomb?"

Poker isn't the only one who wants answers. We've been in church for a half hour, and most of it's been spent voicing our rage and shock at this morning's attack. It takes balls to do what the Wingless Angels did, and they're showing their ability to be a true threat.

We all stare at the remnants we managed to gather and spread out on the table. Tracer's been studying it and inputting data into his laptop, hoping to figure out more about its creator.

"Blain was on duty at the gate last night," Crow states. "I've got Python questioning him in the Nightmare Room. I'm guessing he drank too much and passed out, but we've gotta rule out that he's a mole for those fuckers."

"He's done prospecting, though, right, Pres?" Fudge asks.

"Damn straight. I can't have that kinda laziness in my club."

"While Python deals with Blain, the rest of us need to figure out our next move," I snarl. "Stone and his boys have been quiet for a while, but that's all changed. We fight fire with fire."

"No matter what we decide to do, we're gonna need Addi's help," Ghost says. "If we're gonna get to him, we need an inside man… or woman."

"He's right," Crow agrees. "All in favor of me inviting Addi to the table, thump twice."

As soon as the vote passes, Crow instructs Fudge to go get Addi. The two of them return a few minutes later, and it's clear Addi's surprised to be included.

"I knew this day would come," she says excitedly. "Whaddya need from me?"

"Slow your roll, Ace," Crow says with a chuckle. "Have a seat."

Any guest permitted within these four walls during church knows that you sit at the opposite end of the table as the president. That's just how it goes. But not Addi. She strolls right up to me, grabs my arm to yank me to my feet, and sits down in my place.

"You're lucky he loves you so much," I mutter. "Crow'd have my ass if I did to you what I'd do to anyone else right now."

Rather than be intimidated, Addi rolls her eyes. "You don't scare me."

I open my mouth to set her straight, but one glare from Crow has me moving to Python's empty chair and sitting.

"Smart," Crow quips. "Now, let's get to work. We've identified as many of the Wingless Angels as we can, and taking them all out is a matter of a coordinated effort. I've already texted Shuffle from Limitless Throttle, and they'll help with that. What I can't figure out is how to get to Stone."

"Now I get it," Addi says. "You need me to do that, don't you?"

"Unless I subject one of my men to a prison sentence, yeah."

"It's not gonna be easy," she informs us. "And whatever you want me to do, it can't happen overnight. Not if we want to stay under the radar."

"Any thoughts on how to make it work?" Ghost asks. "I'm thinking a prison transport somewhere is our best bet, but not sure if you wanna go down that road or not."

"I'll check and see if he's got any court appearances coming up, although I doubt it since he already used his last appeal."

"Are there other options for a transport?" I ask. "Is that something you can make happen?"

"You know as well as I do that it takes a lot of coordination for a transport, but I'm sure I can make it happen. It's just gonna take time, like I said."

"What time frame are we looking at?" I ask. "A few days, a week at most?"

"Try a month, at least," she counters. "I don't work at the prison, so it's not like I have direct access. I can pull it off, but I still have to operate within certain limits."

"That's not good enough," I snap. "A lot can happen in a month."

"Yeah, it can," she agrees. "Which is why you all need to do whatever it is that you do and leave me to what I do."

"Thanks, Ace," Crow says. "If you can start on that tomorrow during your shift, that'd be great."

"You're welcome."

Addi doesn't need to be told when she's being dismissed. She's good at picking up clues. After she leaves, I return to my chair.

"That killed you, didn't it?" Screamer taunts.

"Fuck yes, it did," I huff out. "This is my spot."

"Grow up," Crow snaps. "Back to business."

"Let's say Addi can get things arranged," Tracer begins. "How're we gonna get Stone from the transport vehicle?"

It takes an hour, but we come up with a solid plan. Once that's complete, Crow gets Shuffle on the phone, and a unified effort is organized for the Wingless Angels on the outside of a jail cell.

"Church dismissed," Crow says once all votes are complete, and he's confident we've done all we can.

Tracer, Crow, and I remain in the room once the others leave.

"Bro, give us a minute?" I say to Tracer. "I need to discuss something with Pres."

"Yep." Tracer moves to the door. "Don't touch any of that shit. I wanna keep studying it."

"We won't," I assure him.

As soon as the door closes, Crow faces me. "What's up?"

"Wren's gonna ask me what our plan is."

"Probably, but it's club business. You know the rules."

"I do, Crow, and I'm still asking you to bend them a little in this case."

"Why should I do that?"

"Think about it," I begin. "Wren has multiple personalities. What if one of them takes over and hears something they shouldn't or gets the sense that I'm lying? I can't do that to her."

"Jesus, that's a lot to digest," he mutters.

"Tell me about it." I chuckle, but there's little humor behind it. "I'm trying to do right by her, and that means doing right by every part of her. I can't lie. I won't."

"Yeah, yeah. You've made it clear you've got no problem leaving the club."

I rear back as if he punched me. "Do you think that's what I want?" I demand. "Because it's not. This is my home, and you all are my family. But Wren matters, and when it comes right down to it, I'd survive without the club, but I won't without her."

"I get it, I really do," he says. "It's how I feel about Addison. Thank fuck she never asked me to choose."

"Wren isn't either."

"I know."

"So, can you bend the rules, just this once?"

Crow heaves a sigh. "Yeah. You can fill her in. But make it *very* clear that the information doesn't leave her mouth. And do the same with each of her alters if you have to."

"I will… all thirteen of them."

"Thirteen?"

"Yep."

"Shit. You already had my respect, J, but you've got it in spades now. I don't know how you're gonna do this."

"Same way you make it work with Addi. One day at a fucking time."

CHAPTER 24
WREN

As long as I'm breathing, you'll never win.

"Are you sure about this?"

After Journey explained the club's intentions for my dad, I called Dr. Young and moved my appointment up so I could talk to her about it. Surprisingly, Journey came with me. The session went well, but I realized that, while I'm okay with my dad being killed, he's still my dad. I've got things to say to him before it's too late.

Which is how I find myself sitting in the backseat of the club's Jeep in the prison parking lot. Journey and Crow are with me, and I'm grateful for their presence, but the voices won't quiet down, and I'm terrified that I'm gonna switch during this visit.

If you switch, you switch. Show that asshole what he's done to you.

"Addi's positive about a guard being right there the whole time?" I ask for probably the tenth time since we left the clubhouse.

"She is," Crow confirms. "And we'll be there, too. She arranged for a private room that's usually reserved for attorney meetings."

"Right. That's why Journey's dressed like that." I stifle my laugh at Journey's sour expression.

Crow, however, has no such problem. He glances at Journey and cracks up. "I gotta say, a suit and tie is not your look."

"No shit," Journey snaps. "But one of us had to pretend to be a lawyer, and you sure as hell weren't volunteering."

"She's your girl, not mine," Crow says.

"As fun as it is to watch the two of you argue," I interrupt. "I'd really like to get this over with."

Both of them immediately turn serious, all traces of humor gone. Crow is the first to exit the Jeep, and when I reach for my door handle, Journey twists to reach back and stop me.

"Remember what Dr. Young said," he says. "If you wanna leave, we leave, no questions asked."

"Right."

"And I'll be right next to you the entire time."

"Okay."

"Wren?"

"Yeah?"

"You got this."

Journey bleeds confidence, and I soak it in. "Let's go."

He gets out and opens my door for me. As the three of us walk to the entrance, Journey fiddles with his tie but also keeps an arm around me, which is good because I'm pretty sure I'd fall down if I didn't have his support.

It takes a few minutes to get through security, but all too soon, we're escorted to a room where we're instructed to wait.

"Breathe," Journey encourages. "In, out, in, out."

Crow gives me a reassuring smile. "He can't hurt you here."

Before I know it, the door swings open, and a guard leads my dad in and shackles him to the table.

"I'll be just outside the door if you need me," the guard says before leaving us all alone.

My dad glares at us. "Not a one of you is my damn lawyer."

The man sitting across from me is not the man I remember from my childhood. I can tell he's my father, but he's a diminished version of him.

How the hell is he running an MC and causing so much devastation?

I clear my throat. "You don't recognize me, do you?"

Ryan Abbott stares at me with narrowed eyes. "Should I?"

"Cut the bullshit," Journey snaps. "I don't buy this act for a second."

Slowly, a sinister smile spreads across my dad's face. "It's nice of you to visit, Wren."

"Gotta say, I was expecting someone more… I don't know," Crow comments dryly. "Just more."

"Is that right?" Dad asks. "You're exactly what I was expecting, Crow. Young and dumb." He shifts his attention to Journey. "And you… She'll figure it out soon enough."

"Figure what out?" Journey asks.

"That you're cut from the same cloth as her old man."

"He's nothing like you!" I shout, shooting to my feet. The guard knocks on the window, and I take a deep breath before sitting back down. "He's nothing like you," I repeat.

"Keep tellin' yourself that. You were only five when I was hauled away, so I'm sure you don't remember a lot, but trust me when I say you don't know shit about shit." He folds his hands as best he can on top of the table. "Why are you here?"

"Because, for reasons I'll never understand, your daughter wanted to see you before you die," Journey says.

Dad chuckles. "I'm pretty sure it's the Soulless Kings losing this war. Or was that bomb not proof enough?"

"You're the one behind bars, old man," Crow counters. "Not sure how you're gonna manage to win when your entire crew is eliminated."

"Won't ever happen."

"No?" Journey taunts. "Several of your prospects are being taken out as we speak. And more will take their last breath every day until it's your turn."

My dad's cocky glare dwindles, but he quickly masks the fear. "It's cute that you think so. I'm guessing my daughter hasn't explained to you exactly what I'm capable of, prison bars or not."

"Oh, I know all about what you did to your wife and son," Journey says. "But those were the actions of a coward."

Dad moves his head from side to side, popping his neck. "I think this visit is over. Guard!"

The guard opens the door, but I lift my hand to stop him. "We just need a few more minutes. Please?"

He nods and closes the door.

"I've spent the last twenty years dealing with the aftermath of your reign of terror," I snarl. "You're gonna sit here while I say what I have to say, and you're not gonna open that filthy fucking mouth of yours again."

"Oooh, my girl's got a set of brass titties," he taunts.

Journey lunges across the table and lands a blow to my dad's face. It draws the attention of the guard, but apparently, he's not a fan of Ryan Abbott because he simply grins and looks away.

"She told you to keep your goddamn mouth shut," Journey barks.

I tug on Journey's suit jacket, and he returns to his chair. "Thanks, but I've got this," I tell him, then I return my focus to the devil incarnate. "The things you did to mom and Ryan Jr… I'll never forgive you for that. You took away the only goodness in my life, destroyed my innocence, and shattered my mind beyond repair. But guess what, *Dad*? I'm still fucking standing."

"Of course, you are," he sneers. "You've got my blood running through your veins."

"A fact which can never be changed, unfortunately. But I've also got mom's blood, mom's spirit. And as long as I'm breathing, you'll never win. Not against the Soulless Kings, and certainly not against me." I take a deep breath. "Guard!"

My dad sputters a string of curses when the guard lets us out of the room. I block out the sound of his voice as I walk down the long corridor with my head held high and Journey and Crow at my back.

I don't know what awaits us as a result of this visit, but whatever it is, we can handle it. *I* can handle it.

Hell, I just faced my worst foe and came out whole without ever switching.

CHAPTER 25
JOURNEY

I'M HERE NOW.

"For the love of God, would you sit down?"

After taking Crow back to the clubhouse, Wren and I hopped on my bike and came to her apartment. We're gonna stay here tonight, where she's most comfortable. Today was a big day, and it's bound to catch up with her at some point.

"Sorry," I mumble as I sit on the couch next to her.

"Journey, I'm doing my best not to fall apart," she says. "But you pacing for the last half hour isn't helping."

"You're right." I pull her onto my lap and wrap my arms around her waist. "What can I do to make it easier?"

Wren slides her arms around my neck. "I can think of a few things."

She presses her mouth to mine, sliding her tongue along the seam of my lips. I open up for her, reveling in her minty taste.

My hands find their way under her leggings, and I palm her ass cheeks. She grinds her hips, but before I can stand and carry her to the bedroom, she pulls away and grins.

"That's gonna have to wait," she purrs.

"Cock tease," I accuse, adjusting myself.

"I'll make the wait worth it, but…"

"But what?"

"Can we talk first?" she asks tentatively.

"We can do whatever you want."

Wren crawls off my lap and moves to sit so she can face me, curling her legs beneath me.

"I was really scared this morning at the prison," she blurts.

"I know you were, but you did great."

"I did, didn't I?"

"How is it that you turned out to be as amazing as you are?" I ask, genuinely curious. "You could've easily let all of the obstacles you've faced weigh you down, but you didn't."

She shrugs. "I never really thought about it, I guess. Nothing can erase what he did to my mom and brother or change how my mind chose to cope, so I deal with it the best I can."

"Stone was right about one thing."

She stiffens. "What?"

"You sure do have a brass set on you," I say with a grin.

"I wanted to slap him when he said that, but you beat me to the punch… literally." Wren takes a few deep breaths. "Did you notice that I didn't switch?" she finally asks.

"I did."

"Why do you think that is? I mean, that whole visit was one giant trigger."

"Why do *you* think you didn't?" I counter.

She rests her head on the back of the couch and thinks for a moment. "As scared as I was, I knew you wouldn't let anything bad happen. And if you couldn't stop it, Crow would've."

"We will always have your back."

"We really could work, couldn't we?"

"That's what I've been trying to tell you," I jest, tapping the tip of her nose.

"I can't promise you won't have to keep telling me."

"I can do you one better. I'll keep showing you."

"Do you think my dad will make another move soon?" she asks, getting serious.

"Honestly, I don't know. I think he's cocky enough to try, but smart enough to wait for the perfect time."

"Which is when?"

"Never," I assure her. "We're ready, Wren. Whenever he chooses to strike, we're always gonna be ready."

"What if he tries something here? He knows where I live."

"He might." I level my gaze on her. "Maybe you should move into the clubhouse with me."

I expect her to think about it, but she immediately shakes her head. "No. I can't, Journey. Don't get me wrong, everyone is great, but it's a lot for me to try to deal with on a daily basis."

"I could move in here, if that would make you feel better," I suggest.

"I love my apartment, but it's too small for two people."

"Sounds like you're not opposed to the idea of us living together."

"I'm not, not really. It just needs to be the right circumstances."

"And those would be?"

"Well, a bigger place for one. A house that's closer to the clubhouse and where I can have an art studio would be good." She sits a little straighter. "Oh, and a big yard. I'd love to get a dog."

"When you dive in, you dive all the way down to the bottom of the deep end," I tease.

Wren shrugs. "Go big or go home, I guess. I'm not saying I want to buy a house and get hitched or anything. But we could rent something together. That way, we'd both have an out if things go bad."

"Ah, there's the skepticism I've grown accustomed to."

"I don't mean to be a downer, but this is a big step for both of us. I've never opened up to someone like I have with you, and I'd feel better knowing that you're not trapped. Besides, what happens if one of my alters decides they hate you? I mean, I can't control that."

"That won't happen, but I get what you're saying." I rub my fingers over her arm, watching as goosebumps break out across her flesh. "While we're on the subject… Can you tell me about your alters?"

"That's a loaded question, but sure, I'll try."

"If you're uncomfort—"

"It's not that. I'm just not familiar with all of them. Some I'm aware of, but others I only know about because Dr. Young has told me about them."

"So, which ones are you aware of?"

"Well, there's Drew, who's pretty quiet most of the time and very artistic. He'll work on my illustrations when he comes to the front," she explains. "Then there's Vixen and Mavis. Both of them are sluts, and I've had more than one awkward encounter because of them."

The thought of her out in the wild as a slut sends jealousy coursing through my veins, but I say nothing about it. It's not her fault. "I met Mavis," I tell her. "At Ballinger's. That's what led me to dig a little deeper into you."

"Seriously?"

"Yep. She's a trip."

"She's something, yeah." Wren shakes her head. "Anyway… There's Dotty, CJ, Autumn, Mimi, and Rose. I've heard all of them at one point or another. And when I come back to the front, it's pretty easy to tell which of them I am, based on how I'm dressed or what I'm drinking. Sometimes, I look like a schoolmarm and am drinking tea, and other times I'm wearing clothes for a teenage boy and drinking Mt. Dew."

"That's wild."

"Tell me about it," she huffs. "I hate tea, and I feel like I'm suffocating when I come to wearing a blouse buttoned all the way to the top."

"Okay, so those are the ones you're aware of. What about the ones you're not?"

"Dr. Young has told me about Peg, who seems to be like the dorm parent. She rules the roost, so to speak. Then there's Kirby and Annie, two young kids who are best friends, and—"

"Aaron."

Wren's eyes widen. "Please tell me you only know him because of something you read."

"Nope," I admit. "I met him the day you came to the shop to confront me about going to your therapist's office."

"Oh my God," she breathes. "Did he hurt you? Dr. Young told me he's violent."

"Wren, sweetheart, look at me. I'm me, and he's physically you. He didn't hurt me. He sure tried, though. I think it pissed him off that he couldn't."

"That sounds about right. He's tried to strangle Dr. Young before. I don't know what specifically triggers him, but I'm never aware of him beyond a voice in my head sometimes."

"I think he's dubbed himself your protector. That's the impression I got. And I don't think he's appeared since I told him I was taking over that role."

"Huh."

"Maybe that alter has been resolved," I suggest.

"How do you know about that?"

"I've done a lot of research since I learned that you have Dissociative Identity Disorder."

"Really?"

"Of course. How else am I going to know what to expect or how to help you?"

"Where have you been my whole life?" she asks dreamily.

"Doesn't matter where I've been, only that I'm here now."

CHAPTER 26
WREN

I wish Journey could save me like he promised.

One month later…

"That's the last of it."

I smile gratefully at Jackyl as he sets the last moving box on the floor in the bedroom. He and Leah have been helping me and Journey all day, and I know they've gotta be exhausted. Other club members also helped, but as Journey put it, club business doesn't stop just because we're moving.

"I can't thank you enough for all your help."

"I'll thank him for you," Leah purrs when she steps into the room behind him and slaps his ass.

Jackyl spins around and lifts Leah over his shoulder. "How 'bout you thank me now? We've got the moving truck for another hour or so."

"You can do better than that," Journey comments when he enters.

"Really? You don't mind if we use one of the bedrooms?"

Journey slaps Jackyl upside the head. "No, dipshit. You don't get to christen anything before we do. But at least take Leah to the clubhouse to fuck her."

Leah wiggles out of Jackyl's hold. "I don't know. I mean, there's something kinda hot about doing it in places where you shouldn't."

"See, she's cool with it," Jackyl says.

"I think it's time for you two to go," I suggest. "All this talk of sex has me ho—"

"Do *not* finish that sentence," Journey growls. "No one needs to hear it but me."

"Are all of you this possessive?" I ask.

I've spent plenty of time with the club, but there aren't a lot of actual relationships other than Crow and Addison, me and Journey, and Jackyl and Leah. It also doesn't help that sometimes it's not *me* hanging out with them, so I miss stuff.

But on the bright side, no one has made me feel crazy or given me a hard time about switching. They all take it in stride, as if it happens to everyone.

"Yeah, we are," Journey admits.

"Okay, we're outta here," Leah says, dragging Jackyl into the hallway. "We'll return the truck for ya."

"Thanks," I call after her.

As soon as the front door of our rental house closes, Journey scoops me up into his arms and carries me to the mattress that's still on the floor in the master bedroom. He tosses me down and pounces.

"Finally," he grumbles before fusing his mouth with mine.

An hour later, we both shower and put on comfy clothes so we can start unpacking.

Our first night living together is uneventful, and I find I like it that way. I expected there to be awkward silences, or things we'd both do to get on the other's nerves, but that didn't happen. Instead, it's as every day of our lives has led up to us living together.

This morning, we're heading to my agent's office to turn in the sketches I've done for the book about the little girl and the biker. Journey was gracious enough to let me use him as inspiration. Granted, it usually led to other more *adult* activities, but it all worked out.

"You wanna come to the clubhouse with me for a while?" he asks when we leave my agent's office.

"I've got some things to take care of there before I can head home."

"Sounds good to me," I quip. "But can we stop and get something to eat? I'm starving."

"Absolutely."

We stop at the local diner, each of us getting a burger, fries, and a shake. We talk about what kind of dog we're gonna get because he finally caved on that, and agree we'll go to the animal shelter next week to adopt one.

Journey pays the bill, and I follow him outside to the Harley. A sense of unease pricks my spine, and I glance around to find the source. Seeing nothing that seems to be a threat, I shake off the feeling and chalk it up to having had a busy day so far.

Five miles from the diner, a loud rumble surrounds us, and I realize I shouldn't have ignored my earlier unease.

Shifting my eyes from one side to the other, I take in the motorcycles forming a circle around us. Journey tenses and squeezes my thigh before moving his hand to the handlebars in an effort to maintain control.

Fear washes over me, and I bury my face in his back. I wish I could block out the noise, but between all the bikes and the voices, I might as well be standing next to a tornado siren. It's so loud.

No. No, no, no.

Journey slows down, and I turn my head slightly to see the circle closing in. All of Journey's promises to keep me safe flash through my mind, but I shove the thoughts away. This isn't his fault.

"Pull over!" one of the bikers shouts to be heard over the engines.

"Not fucking happening!" Journey yells.

The biker pulls out a gun and points it at me. "Pull the fuck over!"

I know Journey has his own weapon tucked into the back of his waistband, but he's trying to keep us from wrecking. And with death staring me in the face, I freeze.

Journey slows to a stop on the side of the road. If we were closer to town, we might stand a chance of another driver coming along, but we're far enough in the country that that's not likely.

One of the men on our left jumps off his bike and swings at Journey, knocking him to the ground. He didn't have time to put the kickstand down, so me and the Harley topple over with him.

I scramble out from under the heavy machine, ignoring the pain igniting my nerve endings, and manage to get free just in time to see Journey get pistol-whipped unconscious.

"You're coming with us," a man barks as he grabs my arm and yanks me to my feet.

The voices get louder, but before I slip into the darkness, I force my gaze to the patch on the man's cut. The words Wingless Angels MC mock me in bold green letters.

I'm scared. I wish Journey could save me like he promised.

CHAPTER 27
JOURNEY

Bloodlust fuels me.

Pain stabs my skull, and my body aches as I try to roll over.

Where the hell am I?

I slowly open my eyes, only to stare at the cloudless sky.

The floodgates open, and memories assault me. Riding with Wren to the clubhouse, being surrounded by Wingless Angels fucks, pulling over, and then everything goes blank.

I scramble to my knees, but hesitate when a wave of nausea rolls through my stomach. Fortunately, my lunch stays put, and I manage to get to my feet. My Harley is on its side but appears drivable, and Wren is nowhere in sight.

"Motherfucker!" I shout, pulling my cell out of my cut, praying it's not busted.

I call Crow, righting my bike while I wait for him to answer.

"Where the hell are you?" he asks by way of greeting. "Thought you'd b—"

"Wren's gone," I snap. "WAMC bastards forced us off the road and knocked me out."

"Jesus fucking christ," Crow mutters. "Can you make it to the clubhouse, or do you need to be picked up?"

"I can make it. While you gather the officers, can you get Addi to move up Stone's transfer? I know it's set for next week, but we can't wait that long. Wren can't wait that long."

"I'll see what she can do," he assures me. "Just get here."

I disconnect the call, throw my leg over the seat, and start the engine. Gravel spits behind me as I peel off the side of the road, gunning it to get to the clubhouse.

"Meeting room," Conner says when I burst through the front door.

"Thanks."

Crow, Ghost, Screamer, and Poker are standing near the table when I step into the room, the door banging against the wall when I shove it open.

"What'd Addi say?" I demand.

"She's working on it. Since she set it up as him being taken to a police station to be interviewed about an old crime, she thinks she can pull it off that the lawyers had a change in schedule. She'll let me know as soon as she can."

"Okay. If she can't get him out of the prison, I'll just have to go in," I say.

"You know that's not how it works," Ghost snaps. "Even if you got arrested today, you wouldn't be placed in that facility. Not so soon."

"I'll figure something out. There's no other option."

"I'm sure there's a delivery or something we can weasel our way into," Screamer comments. "We're gonna get her back, Journey."

"There's only six Wingless Angels left," Poker reminds me. "Between us and Limitless Throttle MC, we've taken out the rest of them."

"And all six of them were there when Wren was taken," I bark. "Goddammit! This can't be happening. I promised her she was safe with me."

"Journey, brother," Crow says calmly. "You need to focus. You're no good to anyone if you don't get your head on straight."

"Besides, Wren's a strong chick," Poker adds. "She'll get thr—"

Crow's cell rings, and we all stare at the device in his hand. He answers it and puts it on speakerphone.

"Whaddya got for me, Ace?" he asks.

"I now owe some favors, but Stone will be transported out of his current facility to my jail in an hour. I'll send you the route the vehicle will take."

I breathe a sigh of relief. "You're the best, Addi."

"Listen, the guards transporting him will be heavily armed, and they're good men. If you could do this with as minimal damage to the good guys as possible, I'd appreciate it."

"Consider it done," Crow assures her. "Gotta go. Love you."

He disconnects as she's replying. Poor guy's gonna pay for that later, but that's his problem. I've got enough on my plate without worrying about his love life.

Crow's phone dings with a notification. "God, we're gonna owe her big. Addi just sent the route."

"Can you connect it to the projector so we can see it better?" Ghost asks.

Crow does that, and we all crowd around the screen. We discuss several different plans of attack until we settle on the one that will result in less danger to 'the good guys'.

"While you, Ghost, and Poker grab Stone," Crow

says to me. "We'll be here, ready to ride out as soon as we have a location."

"And you've got Shuffle and his boys on call, right?" Poker asks.

"Yeah. They're on standby, waiting for my call."

"Okay." I nod, finally feeling like I might be able to salvage this day afterall. "We ride out in five. Grab all the weapons you can, and meet me out front," I order Poker and Ghost.

Exactly five minutes later, we're pulling away from the clubhouse. Bloodlust fuels me, the drive to get to Wren as powerful a motivator as I've ever experienced.

CHAPTER 28
WREN

With any luck, Wren will be able to walk outta here fairly unscathed.

"What is her problem?"

I shrink into the corner of the room, making myself as small as I can. The couch is missing so it's not the best hiding spot anymore, but the men who brought me here are blocking my path to the stairs. Otherwise, I'd run to my room and hide in my closet.

"According to Stone, her fuckin' brain's broke."

I try to tune them out as they talk about a guy named Stone. The name sounds familiar, but I don't know from where.

I can't believe Journey let them take me.

A phone rings, and the man who's in charge answers it. His voice is muffled as he walks into the kitchen, so I slowly turn my head to take in the guy standing near the front door.

"You sure are pretty," one of them says as he kneels in front of me. When he tries to touch my face, I slap his hand and instantly regret it when he slaps me back. "Seems you're not as broke as your daddy said. But I can fix that."

He stands to unbuckle his belt, but before he can shove his pants down, he's hit from behind.

"Ouch," he cries. "What the fuck was that for, Jester?"

"Slime, you heard Stone. She's not to be harmed."

"Fuck Stone. What's he gonna do from his cell?"

"Kurt's breaking him out today, dumbass. That's why we're doing all this."

"Yeah, whatever. Stone's been behind bars since the club's inception, and we've heard it all before. I'll believe he's gettin' out when I see him out. And I thought this was gonna be more fun," the guy who slapped me complains. "Instead, all we've got are stupid rules to follow."

"And rules will keep us alive, Slime. Or do you wanna end up like the others? Because mark my words, Stone'll make that happen if she's not in one piece when he gets here." He glances at me and scowls. "Take her upstairs. I'm tired of lookin' at her."

Before any of them can grab me, I lunge to my feet and run past them and up the steps. I wait for their dirty hands to grab me, but they don't, and I can only assume that it's because I'm going where they want me anyway.

When I reach my bedroom, I slam the door closed and race to my closet. None of my toys are here, and neither is any of my furniture, but it doesn't matter. As long as the closet door still closes and the hidden latch my mommy installed for me still works, I'll be safe.

I crawl into the small space, turning to press my back to the wall. There's still some sunshine coming through the curtainless windows of my room, so I search for the hidden latch before I close the door. When I come up empty, tears spring to my eyes.

Did Daddy find the latch and take it away?

It's gonna be okay, Annie.

Kirby's voice soothes me. I wish he could be here with me. At least then, we could play a game or something to take my mind off of the men downstairs.

You don't need Kirby.

"I knew he couldn't hack it," I snarl, rage burning through my veins.

I wipe away the little girl's tears and rise to my feet. I'll be damned if I'm gonna hide away in some dingy closet and wait for another man to come rescue me. I'm no damsel in distress.

I'm also not stupid. I can't go downstairs, guns—or no guns, in this case—blazing and expect to wipe out all six of the twats who kidnapped me. No… I need a plan.

I make my way to the top of the steps, careful not to cause any creaking of the floorboards. The voices I heard from earlier waft through the air, and I strain to listen to what they're saying.

"… the hell happened?"

"Kurt went to get Stone from his cell, and he was gone. Apparently, he's being transported to a police station for questioning on a crime from years ago. How Kurt missed this, I don't know, but he's never gonna earn a patch now. Shit, it's a toss-up if he'll live at this point."

"What the fuck are we supposed to do with the bitch?"

"We'll have to improvise. Kurt did manage to get the route Stone's being taken on, so, Slime, you take Rocker and Cowboy to hijack the transport. I'll stay here with Southpaw and Dirty Boy to keep an eye on Wren."

"Can we at least do some damage to the assholes driving Stone?"

"Do whatever the fuck you want with 'em."

"Thanks, Jester," the biker called Slime says. "Let's ride out, boys."

The front door opens and closes, and the three remaining men pass by the bottom of the steps. I flatten against the wall so they can't see me, and when they're out of my line of sight, I move to the room Wren's parents used when they still lived here to see if any of her dad's weapons are still around. It's a long shot, but a long shot is all I have.

"Fuck," I mutter when I find his stash spot empty.

I glance around the room, and my eyes land on the curtain rods. Not my weapon of choice, but like the pricks downstairs, I have to improvise. Once I've collected all the curtain rods from each room, I return to the top of the steps.

With any luck, Wren will be able to walk outta here fairly unscathed.

CHAPTER 29
JOURNEY

We can patch him up and then send him straight to hell.

"You've gotta be kidding me."

I shift my gaze from the road to Poker and then follow his line of sight. Three bikers are riding toward us, and I recognize them instantly from earlier. Seething rage floods my system.

"What the hell are they doing here?"

"I'm guessing the same thing as us, but for very different reasons," Ghost says.

"You two go handle them," I order. "Fuckin' kill 'em. I'll text Crow to send someone to clean up."

They move to the center of the road, pull out their guns, aim, and fire. One by one, three bikers fall from their motorcycles to bleed out on the ground.

Easy peasy.

I glance around to make sure there's no witnesses while they drag the corpses and bikes into the brush on the side of the street. Not much we can do about the blood, but at least there's not dead bodies out in plain sight.

Two minutes later, and with a text sent to Crow, the transport vehicle comes into view. Ghost, Poker, and I move into their path and point our weapons. If we do this right, it should seem like a carjacking instead of a kidnapping. Of course, the masks covering our faces help, and we left our cuts at the clubhouse. We don't care if we're identified, but Addi does since she wants to keep her job.

As Addi explained, the driver pulls the van to the side of the road, and both he and the other guard get out. I guess that's protocol in situations like this. Stupid as hell, if you ask me.

Ghost pulls zip-ties from his pocket as he walks toward them. "Put these on," he demands, tossing them to the men.

"I assume there's a third guard in the back," I state.

"A guard and a very dangerous prisoner," the driver confirms.

I can't stop my grin from spreading. "Exactly what we're counting on."

Once they're secure, Ghost and Poker move to the

rear of the van to open the doors. I follow as I take deep breaths to center myself. I'm itching to put a bullet between Stone's eyes, but I need him alive to find Wren.

"I don't want no trouble," the third guard says as soon as the doors open.

"Neither do we," Poker states. "Go over there with your buddies."

"Wait," Ghost says and grabs the guy's arms to yank them behind his back and zip-tie his wrists. "Okay, now you can go."

Stone strains against his restraints, but he's trapped. There's no way for him to get free without our help.

I pull my mask down so he knows exactly who he's dealing with.

"You piece of shit," Stone sneers. "Where are my men?"

"Oh, you mean the three asswipes who were supposed to spring you?" I taunt.

"Yeah."

"They're just over there," I reply, nodding toward the bushes. "Dead, of course, but there nonetheless."

"You're gonna pay for this," he threatens.

I jump into the back of the van and pistol whip him. "I don't think so. You're gonna tell me where your thugs are holding Wren, and then *you're* gonna pay."

"I ain't telling you shit."

Ghost pulls his trigger, hitting Stone in the kneecap with a bullet. "Sure about that, grandpa?"

To his credit, Stone doesn't scream or shout in pain. He starts to sweat, and swears under his breath, but for the most part, he's quiet.

That won't last.

"Where is she?" I demand, but he just shakes his head, so I shove my thumb into the bullet hole. "Tell me where she is," I seethe.

A few more well-placed, non-fatal wounds, and I have the info I want.

"You two take him back to the clubhouse in this van and stash him in the Nightmare Room. I'm gonna go get Wren, and we'll meet you there." I hop out of the back as I bark orders. "Oh, and have Jackyl on standby in case she needs medical attention."

"Want Jackyl to look this prick over?"

I shrug. "Sure, why not? We can patch him up and *then* send him straight to hell."

CHAPTER 30
WREN

Why?

"None of them are answering their damn phones."

I've managed to make my way downstairs, but now I'm stuck in the coat closet with the damn curtain rods leaning against the wall. I have to time my attack just right, or I won't be able to take all three of them out.

"They should've been back by now with Stone," Jester snaps. "Dirty Boy, I need you to go—"

"Wren!"

Journey?

"Who the fuck is that?" Jester demands just as the front door crashes open and gunfire erupts.

My knees buckle, and I slide to the floor. I glance around at my surroundings and recognize them as a closet I would hide in sometimes when I was a little girl, but I have no memory of how I got here. The last thing I remember is being on the side of the road after Journey was knocked unconscious.

Silence fills the air, and it hits me that the gunfire has stopped. I'm too afraid to move, so I remain still and wait for some indication that I'm alone.

"Wren, sweetheart, where are you?"

"Journey?" I ask quietly. "Journey, is that you?"

The closet door opens, and light filters in. Journey blocks most of it with his giant frame, and he looks like an avenging angel as he reaches for my hand.

"Come here," he says, pulling me to my feet. I throw myself at him, and he lifts me off the floor. "Are you okay?"

I nod against his chest. "Yeah. I am now."

"Are you sure? Because I can kill 'em again if they hurt you."

Leaning to the side, I spot my captors on the floor, blood leaking from holes in their heads.

"One of them slapped me, I think," I admit. "I don't remember it, but my face is sore like I've been hit."

He pushes me away from him without taking his hands off my arms so he can look at my face. "Motherfuckers," he mutters as he lifts his gun and shoots all three of them in the crotch.

"What was that for?" I ask, curious.

Journey shrugs. "Made me feel better."

I can't help but laugh at the matter-of-fact way he says that. "There were six of them, weren't there?"

"Yep. We got them, too," he informs me. "And your dad is back at the clubhouse."

I stiffen. "Why?"

"Because one bullet to the head is too good for him." He smirks. "Bastard already has a few in his legs, but he's breathing."

"Do I have to see him?"

"Not if you don't want to. But Crow's cool with it if you wanna join in on the fun. After all the man put you through, you deserve some justice."

"Can I decide when we get there?"

"Absolutely."

Facing my father is all I can think about on the ride to the clubhouse, and all too soon, I have to make up my mind.

"What's it gonna be, Wren?" Journey asks as he leads me down the hallway to a steel door. "You can stay up here or come down with me and face your demons."

"What if I switch in the middle of it?"

"Then you do. All I ask is that it's Aaron who comes out," Journey teases. "Dude could help fuck some shit up, I think."

I smack him playfully, knowing he's only kidding around. I've learned to joke about my alters when the mood needs a little lightening.

I think about it for a minute longer before nodding. "I'm in."

Journey presses a kiss to my lips and then leads me through the door and down a set of concrete stairs. We stop in front of a monitor, and when I see my father strung up by chains attached to the ceiling, I gasp.

"This is the last chance to change your mind," Journey informs me. "It's not gonna be pretty in there."

I square my shoulders. "It wasn't pretty when he murdered my mom and baby brother. If I survived that, I can survive this."

"Damn right."

He grabs my hand as he hits a button on the wall, and a door slides open, revealing the Nightmare Room. I've heard stories about it, but seeing it in person is more exciting than I anticipated.

"I shoulda known," my father snaps, blood seeping from a cut on his lip.

His prison jumpsuit is stained red from several wounds on his legs, and if I'm not mistaken, there's also black thread where he was stitched up right through his clothes.

"Jackyl did a pretty good job," Journey comments.

"What was the point of fixing him up?" I ask, genuinely curious.

"Have you ever had stitches without anesthetic?"

"No."

"Trust me, it wasn't a walk in the park."

"Just do whatever it is you're gonna do," my father snaps. "Let's get this over with."

"I don't fucking think so," I bite out, closing the distance between us.

I wait for the voices to start yapping, for the fear to make me tremble, but neither happen. I glance over my shoulder at Journey, and he gives me a reassuring smile.

"You've got this," he says.

"Fucking pussy," Dad accuses. "Letting a bitch do a man's job."

Without giving it a second thought, I haul my arm back and thrust a punch to his gut. He groans, and his body sways as his feet barely touch the floor.

"I've got one question for you, *Stone.*"

"And what would that be?"

"Why?" I ask. "Why'd you kill them that night?"

"You really wanna know?" I nod, and he sneers. "Because I could. I'd just formed Wingless Angels MC, and a wife and kids were only gonna hold me back. You were supposed to die that night, too, but some nosy neighbor called the five-oh when they heard screaming."

"You could've left Ryan alone!" I shout, an image of my baby brother popping into my head. I wish I could remember him with a smile on his face, but the only image my brain has held onto is the one of him under a blanket on the living room floor, blood pooled around his tiny body. "Did you know I thought he was my doll?" I ask. "When the police officer carried me out of the house, I looked over his shoulder and saw Mom. And then I saw Ryan, only I thought he was one of my baby dolls."

"He was as useless as a doll."

I take a deep breath, then another, and another. "He was a child," I seethe. "We both were!"

"Wren?" I whirl around at Journey's voice. "Here," he says as he thrusts a long double-edged knife at me.

I shake my head. "Got a hammer?"

Journey twists to grab a hammer off the wall and then hands it to me. "Will that work?"

"Perfect." I look at my father with disgust. "You're gonna feel what they felt."

"You're forgetting one thing, Wren," he taunts.

"What's that?"

"I don't fear death. Do your worst because at the end—"

His head falls to the side the moment the hammer connects with his skull. A sickening crack echoes in the space, and blood spurts from the contact, covering me. I swing at him again and again, taking out years of fury and fear.

"You can't hurt me," I cry, tears streaming down my cheeks as I bludgeon every inch of his swinging body. "Not anymore, you sick fuck."

I don't know how many times I hit him, but my arms start to weaken, and my blows become less frequent.

"He's dead, Wren," Journey says from behind me.

Still, I don't stop.

After another minute or two, arms wrap around me, and I'm pulled back against Journey's chest.

"He's dead," he repeats. "You're free, sweetheart."

"Free," I mutter. "I'll never be free. I'll always have reminders of what he did thanks to my fucking brain."

"Maybe," Journey admits. "But you did all that without switching. Same thing at the prison. Maybe, together, we can work on resolving your alters. And if not, so be it. I love you, every single part of you, and you're free to be whoever it is you are with me."

Slowly, I turn around and lift my eyes to his. "You love me?"

"I've loved you from the second I spotted you at Ballinger's."

"I…" I swallow past the lump in my throat. "I love you, too."

EPILOGUE

JOURNEY

Sex, sweetheart. Hot, sweaty, dirty sex.
Six months later…

"I now pronounce you man and wife."

Cheers and whistles fill the clubhouse, where the wedding took place. Jackyl and Leah decided to hold all of the festivities here to make things easier. Wren threads her arm through mine and wipes her eyes with the Kleenex I made sure she had before the ceremony started.

I lean over and kiss the top of her head. "Do you wish that was us?" I ask.

"Our time will come," she says. "But for now, I like where we're at."

We're still living in the rental, but we've had one big change: a puppy. And when I say puppy, I mean a hundred-pound Great Dane named Zeus who doesn't have an off switch. We learned the hard way not to leave the door to Wren's art studio open at night, and we have to keep our trash cans hidden, but other than that, he's fit in well.

"Can I get everyone's attention?" Jackyl says, his voice booming with the help of a microphone. The room settles down, and he continues. "I know I was a confirmed bachelor, a lover of *variety*, but Leah showed me the error of my ways." He moves his stare to me and Wren. "Journey, thank you, brother, for being a persistent asshole when it came to Wren. If not for your obsession, I might not have gotten to know Leah as fast as I did." The crowd laughs as intended. "And Wren… I know you and Leah aren't sisters, and Journey and I aren't real brothers, but we're all family. And mark my words, you two will be standing right where we are soon."

"We're good, Jackyl," Wren replies with a laugh. "Don't need a ring or piece of paper to know we belong to each other."

"But you needed that tattoo," I say, feigning indignation.

"Well, yeah. If I'm gonna be part of the Soulless Kings, a tattoo is only fitting."

"She's got a point, brother," Crow shouts.

"And now that I've sufficiently shifted the attention away from us," Jackyl says, grinning at Leah. "We're gonna sneak away for a while. But feel free to liquor up and party! We'll be back to join you soon."

The two of them push through the room, accepting congratulations as they go, and I have no doubt their first hour as husband and old lady is gonna be… eventful.

"Can I get you something to drink?" I ask Wren.

"Nah. I'm good."

She doesn't switch nearly as often as she did before she ended Stone's life, but it happens on occasion, so she's careful under certain circumstances to keep herself in control as much as possible. I join her for her sessions with Dr. Young every other week, and they're going well. The good doc seems to have forgiven me for my earlier transgressions, and she's really helping us work through how Wren's Dissociative Identity Disorder impacts our relationship.

"I'll be right back," I tell her and head to the bar.

"She seems like she's doing well," Crow comments when I step up next to him to wait for Conner to take my order.

"She is," I confirm. "How's Addi holding up?"

Crow and Addi learned she was pregnant two months ago, and at first, she was pissed as hell because she worried how it would impact her ability to do her job.

"She's coming around," he says. "She was stressed for so long that there'd be blowback from the whole transport thing with Stone, and she'd just gotten past that when she got pregnant. But she had a long conversation with her dad, and that helped. For a man who thought so little of women, he sure has come around."

"Glad to hear it."

"Speaking of my better half, I better go track her down. She raced to the bathroom a few minutes ago, her face green. Morning sickness is no joke, J. And guess what? Doesn't only happen in the morning."

I chuckle as he walks away. Wren and I are in a good place, but I'd be lying if I said I wasn't really looking forward to seeing her pregnant with our baby.

"What's taking so long?" Wren asks from beside me.

"Sorry. Got sidetracked talking to Crow."

"What can I get you?" Conner asks.

"Jack and coke for me," I say. "And a Dr. Pepper for Wren."

"Coming right up."

"Is he ever gonna get his patch?" Wren asks when Conner steps away.

"No doubt about it," I quip. "We plan on putting it to a vote soon."

"Good. He busts his ass for this club."

Conner got stuck with cleanup of the Wingless Angels bodies, and the dude did a phenomenal job. He was so quick and efficient, there wasn't a hint of it anywhere in the news or on social media beyond what was reported about the 'carjacking' and Stone's 'prison break out'.

"He does, but enough about him," I say, spinning her into my arms. "Whaddya say we head home after this drink? I don't know about you, but I really want to be doing exactly what the newlyweds are doing right now."

"Oh, yeah?" she counters cheekily. "And exactly what are they doing?"

I grin and then lean close to her ear. "Sex, sweetheart. Hot, sweaty, dirty sex."

She cups my cheeks and presses her forehead to mine.

"Fuck the drinks, Journey."

NEXT IN SOULLESS KINGS MC: MARBLE FALLS, TX

BOOK 3: GHOST

Cover and blurb coming soon!

IF YOU HAVEN'T READ BOOK 1 IN THE SOULLESS KINGS MC: MARBLE FALLS, TX SERIES, NOW IS THE PERFECT TIME!

CROW

Crow...

Growing up in Marble Falls was the very definition of boring. Fortunately, my father was the president of the Soulless Kings MC and when he met his maker, I took over the reins. Now I get to make my own fun.

But my way of life is threatened when a sexy siren walks into my club under false pretenses. She thinks she's clever, but I'm not about to let her take down my family. Holding her hostage might not be the best idea, but it's my only option if I want her to see that the Soulless Kings aren't all bad.

What I don't count on is the intense urge to keep her and make her mine.

Addison…

As the daughter of the Chief of Police, I've always strived to be the son he never had. I want nothing more than to follow in his footsteps, but he doesn't think a woman can handle the job. And I'm going to prove him wrong.

But as the saying goes, the road to Hell is paved with good intentions, and my desire to show my father what I'm made of lands me in a heap of trouble. When I'm forced to remain at the Soulless Kings' clubhouse, I regret the decisions that led me there in the first place.

At least, until I realize that the very people I vowed to take down are the only ones who make me feel like I belong.

PROLOGUE
ADDISON

I'm going to prove to him that a woman can do any fucking thing a man can do.

Nine years old…

"You're going to school."

I stomp my foot and ball my hands into fists at my side. It's take your daughter to work day, and my dad is refusing to take me with him. I'm going to be the only little girl in my class if I can't get him to change his mind.

"But Daddy, I have to go," I plead. "Mona's dad is taking her, and so is Carrie's. All my friends will be gone today."

"Mona's father is a dentist, and Carrie's is a mailman," he says with exasperation. "There's no chance that they could get hurt."

"You're not being fair!"

"I've made up my mind, Addison," he snaps. "Now, go get your bookbag so you don't miss the bus."

Tears spring to my eyes, but I blink them away. Daddy doesn't like it when I cry. Rather than risk him seeing my hurt, I whirl around and run upstairs to my room, slamming the door behind me.

I don't waste too much time on my feelings because it won't do me any good. When Daddy makes up his mind about something, there's no changing it. Not even his little girl can do that.

When I open my door to head back downstairs, shouting reaches my ears. Mommy and Daddy are fighting again… about me. Once I reach the bottom of the steps, I stay close to the wall and eavesdrop.

"I've made up my mind, Sharon," Daddy barks. "Addison is going to school, and that's final."

"This is a rite of passage for a daughter," Mommy cries. "Please, Jack, don't make her miss out on it."

"The police station is no place for a little girl," he snaps.

"So, if Addi were a boy, you'd take her?"

Please don't say yes. Please don't sa—

"Of course, I would," Daddy replies, and my

heart sinks. "What better way to turn a boy into a man?"

I wish I were a boy.

Thirteen years old…

"What's taking you so long?"

I stare at my panties and blink back tears. Crying isn't going to make the blood disappear. It isn't going to fix this.

"Go ahead without me," I tell Mona. "Tell Mrs. Cooper that I'm going to the nurse's office."

"Addi, what's going on?" Mona asks. "Are you okay?"

No! I'm bleeding from my naughty parts.

"I'm fine," I insist. "Seriously, go. I don't want you to get in trouble."

Mona sighs. "Call me later?"

"I will after I finish my homework."

Because that's the rule. No friends, no television, no anything until my homework is complete.

Sometimes it really sucks being the daughter of the Chief of Police.

"Okay. Talk to you later."

Her sneakers slap against the ugly bathroom tile, and the moment I hear the door close behind her, I reach for my backpack and pull out my cell.

Mom will know what to do.

But Mom doesn't answer. I leave her a panicked voicemail, begging her to come pull me out of school.

Breathe, Addison. It's just your period, not the end of the world.

Unfortunately, I'm not prepared. Sure, Mom had that talk with me, and everything I need is at home, but I never actually put the pads in my bag.

Think, Addison, think.

I could go to the nurse's office like I told Mona, but I've seen the phonebooks Ms. Hunt hands out to girls. No way will her *supplies* work.

There's only one option left.

Dad.

After entering his cell number, I hit the green call button and press the phone to my ear.

"This better be an emergency," he grumbles when he answers. "Blood or fire, Addison. Those are the only two things whi—"

"I got my period," I blurt, and heat blazes across my cheeks.

"*That* is *not* an emergency," he snaps.

"It's blood, isn't it?" I sass.

"Don't get an attitude with me, Addison."

"I'm sorry," I mutter with a sigh. "I tried to call Mom, but she didn't pick up. I need you to go home, get me some pads out of the bathroom, and bring them to me."

"Can't you ask one of your friends or the nurse for… something?"

Yeah, I could. But I don't want to.

"Please, Dad," I beg.

He clears his throat. "Where are you right now? Aren't you supposed to be in Algebra?"

"I'm in the bathroom," I shriek. "And I can't come out of the stall."

"Addison, get creative," he orders, much like he does with the officers beneath him. "I can't leave right now for something so ridiculous."

With that, he disconnects the call. Angrily, I stuff my phone back into my bag and yank on the zipper to close that pocket. I return my focus to my panties and try to figure out how I'm going to deal with this.

Addison, get creative.

Dad's words tumble around in my mind until creativity strikes. I glance from the problem to the toilet paper. Then I wrap toilet paper around my hand in an effort to make my own version of a sanitary napkin.

I really, really wish I were a boy.

Twenty-two years old…

"Next, we have Addison McGill."

Applause from the small audience fills the air as I stride toward my father. Graduating from the police academy is a big deal, but the look on Dad's face doesn't convey the excitement buzzing through my system.

I did it. I not only survived the academy, but I excelled. My marksmanship scores are the highest in the class, as are every other score for skills we were tested on.

"Congratulations, Addison," Dad says as he shakes my hand.

There's zero emotion in his voice, zero pride. I've spent my life wanting to be just like this man, wanting to make him proud, and he stands here like a damn robot. At least with me. When he calls the names of the others, the names of all the male graduates, his face lights up.

Right here and now, I make myself a promise.

I'm going to prove to him that a woman can do any fucking thing a man can do.

ALSO BY ANDI RHODES

Broken Rebel Brotherhood

Broken Souls

Broken Innocence

Broken Boundaries

Broken Rebel Brotherhood: Next Generation

Broken Hearts

Broken Wings

Broken Mind

Bastards and Badges

Stark Revenge

Slade's Fall

Jett's Guard

Soulless Kings MC

Fender

Joker

Piston

Greaser

Riker

Trainwreck

Squirrel

Gibson

Flash

Royal

Satan's Legacy MC

Snow's Angel

Toga's Demons

Magic's Torment

Duck's Salvation

Dip's Flame

Devil's Handmaidens MC

Harlow's Gamble

Peppermint's Twist

Mama's Rules

Valhalla Rising MC

Viking

Mayhem Makers

Forever Savage

Saints Purgatory MC

Unholy Soul

Wrathful Malice

Grim's Hell

Shadowy Abyss

Soulless Kings MC: Marble Falls, TX

Crow

ABOUT THE AUTHOR

Andi Rhodes is an author whose passion is creating romance from chaos in all her books! She writes MC (motorcycle club) romance with a generous helping of suspense and doesn't shy away from the more difficult topics. Her books can be triggering for some so consider yourself warned. Andi also ensures each book ends with the couple getting their HEA! Most importantly, Andi is living her real life HEA with her husband and their boxers.

Printed in Great Britain
by Amazon